The Practice Proposal

a Suddenly Smitten novel

The Practice Proposal

a Suddenly Smitten novel

TRACY MARCH

Entangled Publishing, LLC
2614 South Timberline Road
Suite 109
Fort Collins, CO 80525
Visit our website at www.entangledpublishing.com.

Bliss is an imprint of Entangled Publishing, LLC. For more information on our titles, visit www.entangledpublishing.com.

Edited by Stacy Abrams
Cover design by Jessica Cantor

Ebook ISBN   978-1-62266-876-2
Print ISBN   978-1-49448-522-1

Manufactured in the United States of America

First Edition February 2013

*To F.P. and Carp for teaching me a lot about baseball,
and @SEA_Beast38 for the inspiration.*

Chapter One

Liza Sutherland would much rather be in a ballpark than a ballroom, and tonight's black-tie charity gala had gone on way too long. She hoped the who's-who patrons at her table hadn't noticed her fidgeting, rolling the tiny beads on her dress between her fingertips. Which baseball teams had won and lost while she'd listened to big-band music and eaten fancy banquet food? She'd have been fine with a foil-wrapped hot dog with mustard and onions and an umpire calling balls and strikes.

Instead, the emcee stood onstage, waving a large white envelope, teasing the audience. The envelope was the last of a big stack, and everyone was wondering whose name was in it. Everyone but Liza. The gala was almost over, and that was all that mattered to her.

Hopefully she'd get home in time to catch a few highlights on the postgame shows.

The emcee cleared his throat loudly. "And the winner of the grand prize in our silent auction tonight—an evening with the Washington Nationals' All-Star first baseman, Cole Collins—is…" The audience murmured with hushed chatter, while seemingly every woman there secretly fantasized that her name was about to be called.

The emcee tore open the envelope. With a dramatic flourish, he removed the card inside. "Congratulations to... Miss Liza Sutherland."

Liza's stomach did a backflip. *What the...?*

After a split second of stunned silence, the crowd erupted with applause and wolf whistles. She quickly shook her head, heat rising in her face. "I didn't even bid. There has to be a mistake," she said, but the only person who heard her above the noise was her mother, who sat next to her.

Sylvia Sutherland's knowing look immediately solved the mystery for Liza. "You. Did. Not."

Of all people, her mom should understand that she wasn't interested in dating. Not now or ever again. But her mom had probably thought she was doing Liza a favor, encouraging her to get out and "meet another nice young man." In fact, she'd been "encouraging" for much of the last two years. An excruciating two years when Liza had grieved Wes Kelley, her former fiancé, who had been a dedicated Secret Service agent. So dedicated that he'd taken a fatal bullet for a visiting third-world dictator...who was assassinated five months later.

The band began another brassy tune that sounded the same to Liza as all the others they'd played tonight. Thankfully, it sent people hurrying toward the dance floor, diverting attention from her.

"It was for two good causes," her mom said proudly. "You." She squeezed Liza's hand and despite her frustration, Liza relished the warm comfort she'd relied on through her grief. "And the BADD Athletes Foundation."

Her mother had founded the organization several years ago, shortly after she'd been appointed to Major League Baseball's Health Policy Advisory Committee. She practiced sports medicine, loved baseball, and hoped BADD—"Be Aware of the Dangers of Doping"—would make a difference in the lives of young athletes.

Liza felt the same way, and she even worked for the foundation, but she wished her mom would've kept her money to herself tonight. She leaned closer so she wouldn't be overheard. "For starters, I'm not a *cause*. And I don't think it's appropriate for someone who works for BADD to win the grand prize. That wasn't the point of the auction." It was hard enough for her to go to work every day and have to prove she was more than capable of doing her job, regardless of whom her parents were. Now there was this.

"Nonsense." Her mom waved her hand airily. "The point of the auction was to raise money and have a little fun." She winked.

"But you and Dad would have given that money to BADD anyway. If someone else had won the stupid date, we could've had double the funds." Liza was sensitive about fund-raising. It was the part of her job she liked the least and struggled with most.

Her mom grinned. "But *you* won the stupid date, sweetheart."

She just doesn't get it. Liza didn't want a date. She'd had a once-in-a-lifetime romance with Wes, and she'd lost him. Everyone expected her to move on, but grief had its own timeline, and Liza's heart still ached for him. Living with his memory would be her ever after, and she was satisfied with that.

"What makes you think I'd even want to go out with Cole Collins?" The idea alone tied Liza's stomach in a knot.

"Because ever since you met him at your father's camp, you've cherished that autographed baseball he gave you like it was a diamond the same size." Of course her mom remembered all of the most embarrassing times of Liza's awkward teenage life, and seemed determined to remind her of them.

Liza scrunched her face. "I packed that ball away years ago." But she remembered vividly that day at the camp, where she'd hung out for weeks just to watch Cole Collins *breathe*.

Her father had been a professional baseball player. After he'd retired, and before he became co-owner of the Orioles, he ran a summer camp for promising young players. Cole had attended three summers straight.

"I was all knees and elbows, and he was all full-blown ego." Liza shook her head. "The only reason I kept that ball was I hoped it'd be worth something someday." She took a deep breath and blew it out loudly. "I should sell it on eBay."

"You don't need the money, sweetie," her mom said. "And you and Cole aren't teenagers anymore. You've both had your struggles. Maybe he's changed—you certainly have. Just go out with him and have a nice evening."

Liza toyed with one of the straps of her peridot-green cocktail dress. It had been Wes's favorite because it matched her eyes, and it fit "just right." She remembered wistfully how he'd sometimes called her Goldilocks—despite her dark-red hair—because everything about her was "just right" for him. After the love she'd shared with Wes, how could she even think about going out with a guy like Cole Collins…even to raise money for charity?

"I'm not interested in dating, Mom—especially a player like Cole. He's lucky he didn't get arrested last weekend with Nikki Barlow."

Her mom pursed her lips. "I think Cole just happened to be with the wrong wayward starlet at the wrong time. Nikki was the one driving under the influence, and they found the drugs in *her* purse. She's the one who was charged, not Cole."

After the well-publicized drug-related drama Cole had been involved in, there had been some debate at BADD about pulling from the auction the "evening out" grand prize he'd donated. But considering the funds the item was expected to raise, and that Cole hadn't actually been arrested, the auction committee had decided to move forward. Besides, all of the advertising for the gala and auction had included the high-profile listing and had gotten BADD plenty of press.

"You seem pretty quick to defend him," Liza said, careful not to sound accusing. She just wondered why.

"He's hanging around with the wrong people." Her mother was always good for a classic mom-quote. "But I'm giving him the benefit of the doubt." She pulled at a lock of Liza's long hair. "*And* trying to reintroduce him to a nice girl who used to think he was pretty special."

"He's interested in movie stars and models." Liza shrugged. "Not women like me."

"So you've been keeping tabs on his social life?" her mom teased.

"No. All I have to do is flip on *E!*, wait five minutes, and they'll run a clip showing him with some Victoria's Secret model."

"You're as beautiful as any of those girls. And smart, too."

Liza smiled, appreciating the compliment and wishing— not for the first time—that brains translated to curves. "But no one's ever paid me to model sexy lingerie and wear angel wings."

Her mom shook her head, her expression turning serious. "Wes would want you to find love again. He'd want you to be happy."

Liza swallowed the lump in her throat. "What's Dad going to think? The Nats are our rivals in the Battle of the Beltway." She always talked about the Orioles as if she were one of them. "And there's a real possibility the Os and the Nats will go to the World Series this year. That makes things even more uncomfortable right now."

Her mom swept a section of her ash-blond bob from her face and shrugged casually. "It's a friendly rivalry, and your dad will be fine—especially if the Os make the Series." She put her arm around Liza and pulled her close. "He'd be pleased to see you happy."

Happy hadn't been in Liza's emotional repertoire for a long time. She couldn't imagine a date with Cole Collins changing that. "I can't," she said.

The hurt in her mom's eyes tugged at Liza's heart. "If you won't do it for you," she said gently, "will you do it for me?" She gazed at Liza with all of the hope and great expectations that a mother has for her daughter, and Liza knew her mother had suffered, too. Surely she'd felt helpless as she tried to ease Liza's grief in so many ways. From mother/daughter weekends to coming over in the middle of the night to listen and dry Liza's tears. If she could've figured out how to bring Wes back to life, she would have, and sacrificed herself to do it.

Liza really wanted to say no to the date with Cole, but the look on her mom's face wouldn't let her. With a sinking feeling in her stomach, she squeezed her mom's hand and said, "Okay. I'll go."

· · ·

Cole Collins glanced up from his menu and caught the too-cheery young waitress staring at him. He gave her a lazy half smile and left it at that. She was cute enough, and he was all about flirting, but this wasn't the time.

For starters, it was way too early, and he was still half asleep. He didn't have a game until tonight, and he could've slept in if his agent hadn't insisted on meeting for breakfast. So here he was at Ted's Bulletin, an incredibly popular upscale diner on Barracks Row in DC's Capitol Hill. Cole glanced across the booth-for-two at Frank Price, knowing he'd set up this seven thirty breakfast to try to keep Cole from staying out too late last night.

It hadn't worked.

"Are you guys ready to order?" the waitress asked.

Cole nodded at Frank, who was built like a bear and took up every bit of the space on his side of the booth.

"I'll have the beer biscuits and sausage gravy." Frank's Virginia-gentleman baritone carried up into the rusted pressed-tin ceiling. He took a gulp of his Bloody Mary. "With two eggs sunny-side up and hash browns."

"And you, Mr. Collins?" the waitress asked.

Cole bunched his lips. He would have liked her a lot better if she would've just let him enjoy his breakfast incognito.

"I'll have the Walk of Shame burrito," he said.

"Fitting," Frank muttered.

Cole had hesitated to order his favorite breakfast, knowing Frank would have something to say about it, but the sirloin steak, egg, and cheese burrito seemed like the best way to fortify himself against what was coming. He handed the waitress the oversize old-newspaper-style menu.

"Coming right up," she said and headed toward the open-air kitchen at the back of the dining area. Cole would swear she'd put a little extra in the sway of her hips.

Frank's salty remark still hung between them. Cole understood that his agent was pissed about his brush with the law last weekend—hell, he was pissed at himself. This was their first time face-to-face since then. Frank had been remarkably quiet about the situation at the time, and then the Nats had gone on a road trip the next day. Since Frank wasn't one to hash out sensitive issues on the phone, Cole expected to hear what-was-what from him this morning. Frank had always had his back, so Cole felt like he owed the guy the respect to sit and take the ass-chewing he deserved.

It helped that Frank was a seasoned agent—not slick and fake like some of the younger ones—but smart and experienced and wise. The guy could also wrangle some pretty impressive deals. Cole had needed plenty of wrangling to keep himself employed over the years—and possibly over the last week. No doubt Frank's negotiating skills had gone a long way toward keeping him from the front of a mug-shot camera that past Sunday.

"Last night was our lucky night, son," Frank said, his intense gaze leveled on Cole.

Cole couldn't imagine what had been lucky about it. The Nats had lost to the Giants after eleven innings, and with the playoffs right around the corner, this was no time to be losing. But if that's what Frank wanted to discuss, Cole was willing. Talking about last night was a heck of a lot better than talking about last week.

"Lucky how?" Cole asked.

"You see the tweet about the Sutherland girl?"

The guy never missed anything. Sometimes Cole wondered if Frank kept up with him better than he kept up with himself.

Sutherland girl? Cole shook his head.

Frank pulled his iPhone from his pocket and put his beefy fingers to work. He handed Cole the phone just as the waitress arrived with their breakfast.

BADD Athletes Foundation @BADDAthletes
@LizaSutherland wins silent auction date with Nationals' All-Star first baseman @ColeCollins.

#nowthatsaprize

Strange…

"You look confused," Frank said, wasting no time digging in to his heaping plateful of food.

Cole stared at the tweet and let his breakfast sit. "I forgot all about this."

"Well, the timing couldn't be better, considering the stunt you pulled last week." Frank swiped his napkin across his mouth and scowled. "Who would've thought you'd be needing some positive publicity from an antidrug program? I hope BADD took out a front-page ad in the *Post*."

Cole set the phone on the table and rubbed his forehead. This was the conversation he'd been expecting. "The drugs were Nikki's, Frank. Sure, I might've had one too many drinks. That was obvious." He shook his head. "But no drugs. You know that. My test came back clean."

"I know it." Frank stabbed his fork toward Cole. "You know it. And the Nationals know it. But it's the optics, son. And the Nats don't need your kind of trouble. The girls, the booze, the drugs—whether they're yours or not. You're in too deep with all of it."

Cole took a slug of his coffee to keep himself from saying anything else.

"We've got contract negotiations coming up," Frank said. "On the field, you've set yourself up fine—two seasons running. But I was getting questions even before last week about your shenanigans off the field. The Nats' bigwigs think you might be wearing yourself out with all that carousing." He piled his fork full of eggs and hash browns and held it just above his plate. "Then you went and pulled that stunt with Nikki what's-her-name, and almost got yourself arrested. You're giving 'em plenty of reason to worry that you won't be a good investment long-term."

"They're seeing things as worse than they are," Cole said defensively, knowing he was wrong. The Nats were big on high-character players, and a lot of his teammates were settled with wives and kids. The owners worked hard to keep everything classy, from the front office on down. They were all like one big family, but Cole was the black sheep right now.

"I think they're seeing things twenty-twenty," Frank said firmly. "And they're the ones with the ball club. They can contract whomever they want. They've come across guys like you before, and they've been burned once or twice."

"We can go to a different team," Cole said without conviction.

Frank lowered his thick eyebrows. "The Nats might be heading to the World Series this year—I'm seeing a pennant at worst. You want to leave a team on that kind of high?"

Cole shook his head. He and Frank both knew he didn't want to leave the Nationals. They'd all busted their asses to get as far as they had, and he was lucky to be there with them. Plus, he'd practically grown up with the Nats. He'd been totally alone after he'd been drafted, but he'd found a home with his team, and the closest thing to a family he'd ever had. He'd struggled for seven frustrating years, but they'd kept him around anyway, and now he was finally performing.

He'd figured that's all it would take for them to keep him, but clearly he'd figured wrong.

The reality he'd ignored hit him like a hundred-mile-per-hour fastball: he needed the Nationals. He'd never admit it to anyone, but he didn't want to be alone again.

Frank picked up his phone, tapped the screen, and glanced at the tweet. "That's why this date with the Sutherland girl sets up perfect for us."

Cole finally took a bite of his burrito. He couldn't argue

that this was a good time for him to be associated with the BADD Athletes Foundation, but he wondered why Liza Sutherland had surfaced all of a sudden.

He hadn't seen her since they were teenagers—and he was curious how she'd grown up. "Let me see that tweet again." Frank handed him the phone. He tapped the link to Liza's profile, and her picture came up. One glance at her and his pulse fired like a home-run hit headed for the upper deck.

Holy…

The woman he saw looked nothing like the girl he remembered. She had long, dark-red hair, sparkling green eyes, and a pretty, genuine smile. Cole figured her for a city girl, but she had a kind of small-town innocent look that was hard to find anymore. He couldn't believe she was the same girl who'd hung around her father's baseball camp for weeks, just for him.

He read her profile: *Manager of camp operations for the BADD Athletes Foundation.*

So she worked organizing the same kind of camps where they'd met. Cole totally respected that, especially considering all the more glamorous opportunities her parents could've hooked her up with. He winced at the thought of John and Sylvia Sutherland, but he knew better than to dwell on it. His rocky past with Liza's folks had nothing to do with her.

"You don't look too thrilled," Frank said. "The way I see it, we coulda done much worse."

"For sure." Cole stole another glance at Liza's picture. "I'm okay with it." And why wouldn't he be? Liza Sutherland was smokin' hot.

Frank nodded. "The girl's a looker. She's got a good job, a solid family. We can forgive 'em this once for being in the tank for the Orioles." He smiled. Anyone who liked baseball was all right with him—they kept business going and money streaming in.

"No need to worry about her job or her family," Cole said. "It's just one date." He took a bite of his burrito, enjoying the tender steak and creamy cheese, until Frank's raised-eyebrow look made him stop chewing. "What?" he murmured through a mouthful.

"This Sutherland girl works for *drug-free* BADD." Frank took a swallow of his Bloody Mary and licked his lips. "Going out with her will make it look like you're cleaning up your act. Besides, she's our chance to prove you're settling down, at least until we get your contract negotiated."

"Whoa. I'm not sure what you mean by that, but I'm sure I don't like the idea." He gave Frank a serious stare. "Listen, we've already gotten the positive publicity from the BADD donation, and the timing couldn't have been better. One date—we're good. I promise I'll behave after that." He winked.

Frank shook his head and grimaced. "We're talking about your future, son. *Seven years* you've spent toiling your way to the top. You're twenty-nine, and not getting any younger." He shrugged his broad shoulders. "But with two All-Star seasons under your belt, a Gold Glove, and a Silver Slugger, we can name your price—as long as you make it look like your partying-and-playboy days are done."

Cole flinched. "I hear you." *And I know you're right.* He let out a long, labored sigh. "It needs to look like I'm settling down." *At least for a couple of months.*

"Bingo." Frank stared him in the eye. "And it wouldn't hurt your cause if you went and did something traditional like fall in love…propose…get married."

Cole groaned as his stomach knotted. He'd sat down at this breakfast free and single. Before he could even eat a burrito, Frank had him set up on a date, faithful to one woman, in love, engaged, and married. "You're getting way ahead of yourself, man."

Frank splayed his hands on either side of his plate, straightened his back, and leaned forward. "How badly do you want a new contract with the Nats, son?"

Cole raked his hand through his hair and grabbed a fistful of it in the back. After a moment he said, "There's nothing I want more."

Frank tossed his napkin on the table and relaxed in his seat. "Well, there you go."

The waitress stopped by and asked, "Anything else for you gentlemen?"

Looking pleased with himself, Frank nodded and smiled. "I'll have a homemade peanut-butter-and-bacon poptart to go."

The thought of eating peanut butter and bacon in the same mouthful made Cole a little queasy. So did the idea of settling down. But after the waitress left, he pushed his plate aside and propped his elbows on the table. "You've never steered me wrong before, Frank. So I'm willing to play along with your plan." He cleared his throat. "But we've got to find a different girl." *Because things are a little complicated between Liza Sutherland's folks and me.* "Liza would never go for this."

"No can do," Frank said without hesitation. "I coulda personally recruited a bunch of ladies and not come up with a more wholesome gal—she's *perfect* for what we need."

Chapter Two

Cole strode into the waterfront condo building on Baltimore's Inner Harbor, his pulse running a little high. If this were any other Friday night off, he'd be looking forward to a stress-free night out at the clubs—comfortable party atmosphere, maybe a casual hookup. There wouldn't be much partying tonight, though, considering the date Frank had arranged. He'd have to get used to the slow life, at least for a little while, and that didn't really bother him, considering what was at stake. What did freak him out a little was this unexpected reunion with a girl he'd only known as a teenager. The scary thing was, Liza might just know him better than any woman he'd ever dated, even though he hadn't seen her in years. He sucked in a deep breath and blew it out with a hiss.

The lobby was all granite and glass, maximizing the water view. Cole caught the attention of the security guard, who looked like a jolly ex-linebacker sitting behind the sleek counter. The guy squinted, then his eyes went wide as Cole came closer.

"I'm Cole Collins, and—"

"I thought that was you!" The guy looked starstruck, but Cole had started to get used to that. "Man, I'm your number one fan."

Cole smiled. He heard that a lot, too, and he never got tired of it. There'd been a time when he'd had no fans at all. *Except Liza.*

"Thank you," Cole said. "That means a lot. I'm...um... I'm here to see Liza Sutherland."

The guard nodded, as if he approved. "I'll buzz her for you."

Cole paced while the guy picked up the phone, punched in a number, and waited.

"Hello, Miss Liza." The guard held the cordless phone with one hand and unzipped a backpack next to his chair with the other. "Mr. Cole Collins is here to see you." He pulled a well-worn Nats baseball cap out of the backpack. "Yes, ma'am." He hung up the phone. "She'll be right down," he said to Cole. "While you wait, would you mind signing my hat?"

"No problem." He signed the cap and gave it back to the guard.

"Don't tell Liza." The guard smiled and nodded. "But I hope you guys win the Series this year."

Cole grinned, hoping they did, too. "One step at a time," he said. "We're focused on making the playoffs right now."

"Oh, you got that, man. You got that."

Cole was fresh out of small talk. He'd suddenly become preoccupied wondering if Liza would look as good in person as she did in her picture. What would she be like now that she was all grown up? He thought back to some of the afternoons at the baseball camp and the conversations they'd had. She'd been easy to talk to because he had placed her squarely in the friend zone, even though she'd seemed to have a different zone in mind. If she still did, maybe easing her into a fake relationship wouldn't be too difficult.

A pang of guilt clenched his stomach. Could he really do

that to her? One of the elevators arrived at the lobby with a *ping*. Cole shifted his gaze to the spotless stainless steel doors as they slowly slid open, and out stepped Liza.

Holy hotness…

The woman was definitely a hell of an awesome sight in 3-D. Any red-blooded man would appreciate her lithe figure and perfectly proportioned curves, accented by a lucky pair of just-tight-enough black jeans. Her fitted sweater looked featherlight and feminine, and it matched her pale-green eyes exactly.

"Here's Liza now," the guard said, nodding as she stepped closer.

Liza smiled at the security guard—she had dazzling white teeth, no longer sporting the braces Cole remembered—then turned to him. "Hello, Cole," she said, her voice as perfect for radio as her face was for TV. He wondered why she hadn't chased a career in either. She held out her hand. "I think we've met." He was captivated for a moment by the sprinkling of freckles across her nose.

Cole grasped her hand and held it for a moment. "It's good to see you again." She squeezed his hand lightly, slipped her hand out of his, and swept a lock of silky cinnamon-colored hair away from her face.

"You look amazing." Cole often said something like this to his dates but couldn't remember ever meaning it quite so much. He swallowed hard.

Color rose in her face. Her gaze locked on him and his heart stammered. He'd swear he saw all the things she knew about him right there in her glimmering green eyes. "Thanks." She grinned and gave him a playful once-over. "You turned out pretty good yourself."

The security guard watched them curiously, making Cole even more uncomfortable.

"You've met Sean," Liza said, giving him a knowing look as if she felt the same way.

Sean nodded, beaming. "He autographed my Nats hat."

Liza shook her head and puckered her shiny, incredibly kissable lips. "You're killing me, Sean."

"She's all about the Orioles," he said to Cole.

Cole grimaced. "I'd imagine."

Liza proudly tipped up her chin. "Go Os."

Cole glanced at Sean, who shrugged and shook his head.

Free-spirited and confident, Liza didn't seem like she'd fall easily into a fake relationship with anyone. But Cole had to make this work. He had to get that contract. What could he do to convince her to stick around for a while?

This is going to be a long night.

• • •

"That's *your* pickup?" Liza's nerves had made her jittery, and she sounded more surprised than she'd meant to that Cole had shown up in a white Ford quad cab. She had taken him for the flashy-sports-car type.

"Yep, she's mine." He walked in stride with her, looking free and easy with his blond hair and blue jeans. At six-foot-four and two-twenty, according to his stats, he was all lean muscle, with long legs and broad shoulders and the grace of a stallion. Unmistakably a powerful athlete, he'd earned the nickname "Crush" from Nats fans because he consistently crushed baseballs out of the park. No wonder he attracted so many women. He was clearly irresistible.

"Then who's the guy in the driver's seat?"

"That would be Mack, our driver." He grinned confidently. "I guess I could've come in a limo, but I'm more comfortable in a pickup." He opened the rear door of the quad cab and gave her a sidelong glance. "So let's call this a hybrid." He winked, his blue eyes shimmering.

A flock of seagulls took flight in her stomach. Liza hadn't seen him up close and in person for years, only playing baseball from a distance or on TV. She'd forgotten about the small mole he had on the cusp of one of his high cheekbones. Her mom might call it a beauty mark, which sounded kind of feminine, but there was nothing girlie about it. The mole looked totally masculine paired with his even features and strong jaw. And he might have had the most perfect lips Liza had ever seen on a man. The thought sparked a twinge of guilt.

Oh, Wes. I hope you're okay with this. It was just one date—bought and paid for by her mother, no less.

Cole helped her into the truck, then walked around to the other side, looking somewhat like the boy she remembered, yet more filled out and manly. She thought about how many years it had been since they'd spent time together. After her teenage crush, she'd kept track of him while he'd been an Academic All-American at UNC, and she'd been busy at college herself. Even so, she hadn't kept in touch. She'd really fallen for him, but she was smart enough to see that he hadn't been all that into her.

"Hello, Mack," she said to the driver, a slender older man with prickly white hair who looked as though he'd spent a lot of time in the sun. "I'm Liza."

"It's a pleasure, miss."

Cole got in, they settled into the cushiony leather backseat of the pickup, and Mack pulled into Friday night traffic. "My Kinda Party" played on the radio, turned down low. "How 'bout a beer?" Cole asked, sounding more relaxed than he had moments ago in front of Sean. He opened the cooler that sat on the floor behind the console, filled with ice and longnecks.

Liza nodded, feeling a little dazed. She hadn't known what to expect on this date, but so far, it was none of the above. A stocked beer cooler in a pickup/limo hybrid with a hired driver named Mack?

Cole grabbed a beer, popped the cap, and handed her the longneck.

"Thank you," she said as he opened one for himself.

Cole raised his bottle. "To auctions for charity."

Heat crept into Liza's face. Her neck was probably getting splotchy, too. She was nervous enough as it was. All she'd needed was a reminder that this was a "charity" date. "Talk about putting yourself out there…"

She tipped her bottle toward his and struck it with a vibrating *chink*.

"That was quite a donation you made to the BADD athletes," he said with a tinge of that Southern accent she remembered.

She stole a quick glance at him. He had one of those unusually beautiful faces that you could get stuck staring at if you let your gaze linger too long. "My mom actually placed the winning bid in my name, and she kind of insisted that I go."

Cole drew his head back, looking surprised and a little confused. His perfect lips quirked down at one corner.

"So if you'd refused to go out with me, I'd be sitting here with Sylvia right now?" He gave her a crooked grin.

"She's one of your biggest fans." Liza grinned back at him, sensing a spark of connection she hadn't felt when they were teens. She quickly warned herself not to be fooled by such a playboy. Plenty of other women had probably imagined a special connection with him, too. There was still a hint of confusion in his eyes. He took a long swallow of his beer and raised an eyebrow. "What about you?"

She bit her lip and smiled coyly. "I'm still undecided."

Chapter Three

The early evening sun shone in the window of the truck and shimmered on Liza's silky hair. Cole had never dated a redhead. And as far as he knew, he'd never dated a woman who hadn't wanted to go out with him. Girls had frequently been available, so he'd rarely had to chase them. Frank could've made things easier on him if he'd picked a girl Cole didn't have to win over. Why had Sylvia Sutherland insisted on Liza going out with him? Liza had known him when he was a nobody, and he wondered if she'd been more impressed by him then than she was right now. The longer she sat next to him, the more uncomfortable he felt about his intentions.

"It's been a long time"—Liza reached into her purse and pulled out an old baseball—"since you gave me this." She bunched her lips, distracting him a little, and handed him the ball.

Cole knew immediately it was the one he'd autographed for her years ago at John Sutherland's baseball camp, where he'd spent the better part of his teenage summers. Cole remembered the first day he'd shown up at camp in Baltimore, thanks to an anonymous benefactor who'd paid for him to go.

He'd been wide-eyed and in awe of Sutherland—the Hall-of-Fame shortstop who had set records and played in three World Series, one as MVP.

John Sutherland had inspired him with his easygoing coaching style. He'd helped Cole sharpen his skills and work on his weaknesses in the game. Even more than that, Sutherland had assured Cole that he had talent *and* the potential to go pro. Just as Cole's father might have done, if he'd had one. And just like his mother might have done, if she could've torn herself away from countless boyfriends long enough to come see him play.

Over the course of three summers, Sutherland became the father figure Cole had always longed for. And Sylvia had treated him special, too. Then, that last summer, Liza had started hanging around. Skinny and awkward but easy-to-talk-to Liza. On the last day of camp, he'd autographed the baseball and given it to her. In hindsight, it seemed like an arrogant thing to do. But at the time, he'd been naive about his future. He'd felt more like a star then than he did today. And Liza, all bones and braces, might've been his first real fan.

He rolled the ball around in his hand, pressing the seams with his fingertips and rubbing his thumb across his carefully signed name. "This might be a collector's item. I can actually read my signature." These days, he signed so many autographs in such a hurry that his signature had become two Cs and a squiggly line.

"Guess I was smart to keep it," she said lightly. He couldn't decide if she was teasing him or not. "I slept with it under my pillow for weeks."

Now that was news, coming from Miss Undecided. But after thinking about it a second, he remembered how smitten she'd seemed with him back then. It was hard to believe the woman sitting next to him and that teenage girl were the same person. "For real?"

"I kind of had a crush," she said shyly. "And I was sure you'd be a superstar." She shrugged. "Turns out I was right."

"That's cool of you to say." He pressed his lips together tightly. "But there's way more to the story than that." It was no secret he had struggled over the years, going from the minors to the major league and back. Becoming a superstar hadn't been the short, happy journey Liza made it sound like. "Would you like to have it back?" she asked, offering up the baseball.

Another first. No one had ever returned something he'd autographed. "You don't want it?"

"Sleeping with it under my pillow gave me a crick in my neck." She grinned.

He lowered his eyebrows. "You never heard of 'The Princess and the Pea'?"

"I can't believe *you've* heard of it," she teased.

Cole remembered his grandma reading the story to him from a thick, worn book when he was a kid. "There are plenty of things about me you might not believe."

She looked at him curiously, a glimmer of mischief in her eyes. "Me, too." He put the baseball in the cup holder, still unsure if her giving it back to him had been an insult or a compliment. He wasn't used to women who kept him guessing, but he thought he kind of liked it.

They had made good time getting out of the city and into the rolling hills of Virginia. After several more miles, Mack turned the pickup off the road and onto a long, winding gravel driveway flanked by lines of magnolia trees. On either side, fields and pastures stretched out until they met the woods beyond. Now that they'd arrived, Cole started to relax a little, but an undercurrent of uneasiness tugged at his conscience.

He wasn't sure he'd be able to get Liza to agree to a second date, much less something longer-term—and fake. Even so, the farm was perfect for what he and Frank had planned.

"This is beautiful." Liza gazed around, wide-eyed, with a hint of a smile, and Cole caught a glimpse of that small-town wholesomeness he'd seen in her Twitter profile picture. She seemed to have relaxed some, too.

Mack stopped the truck in front of a well-kept barn, painted white with a red tin roof. "Y'all wanna jump out here?" he asked. "I'll head around back and hitch up."

Liza furrowed her brow and looked at Cole. "Hitch up?"

He nodded. This time the mischief was in his eyes. He got out of the truck, walked around, and opened the door for her. She stepped down next to him, the scent of her perfume swirling in the air. It was fresh and simple—like a bouquet of wildflowers might smell, not heavy like those perfumes that hung thickly in the clubs where he partied.

As soon as they were out of the truck, Mack drove around the back of the barn. The autumn breeze nipped at Cole's neck as the sun sank lower in the sky. He hoped the sunset would be as postcard-perfect as the farm. He needed Frank's plan to work, after all, whether he felt right about it or not.

Liza turned in a circle, taking it all in. He didn't miss the chance to check out the way her jeans hugged her curves and tapered down her long legs to her sexy-yet-sensible boots. Her silky long hair caught a ray of the fading sunlight, and he imagined combing his fingers through it.

She faced him with her chin tipped up, a little wonder in her eyes. His gaze instinctively skimmed the smooth curve of her neck, dipped quickly to the V-neck of her sweater, and shifted back to her lips. He inhaled sharply. She was fine from every angle, but he wasn't sure she knew it.

"I figured you for more of a swanky-restaurant, glitzy-nightclub kind of guy," she said.

She'd have a better idea of what he was all about from their conversations years ago than she would judging from what she guessed now. Cole was the same guy deep down—still looking for a place to belong.

Most people took him for a high-life kind of guy—and he'd given them every reason to think that. Now it had all backfired, and the one thing that mattered to him was at stake. According to Frank, faking a romance with Liza was just the way to fix things, but now that he was out with her, Cole had even more doubts. Sure, she seemed like an upstanding girl who conveniently happened to work for an antidrug foundation associated with baseball. All that sounded good, but she was also the one girl who might be able to see through him.

He kicked at the dirt with the toe of his boot. "Like I said, there are things about me you might not believe. This could be one of them." He made a sweeping gesture. "I enjoy a night out like this—no limos or chefs or drinks with fancy names. If someone else had won the auction date, that might've been what she got." He gave Liza a sidelong glance, and she looked at him skeptically. "But when I found out it was you…"

Her questioning gaze met his, and he worried that she'd never believe what he was about to say. Man, those pale-green eyes were something. "I just wanted things to be different." Was that really a lie? Frank had suggested the farm for their date, but Cole *had* liked the idea. He tucked his hands into the pockets of his jeans.

With a hint of a smile, she held his gaze a beat longer, then looked away just as Mack strode around the corner of the barn, a satisfied look on his weathered face. "We're good to go 'round back. Anytime you're ready."

"Thanks," Cole said. "We'll be there in a second."

Mack nodded and headed back around the barn.

Cole turned his attention to Liza, "Ready?"

She shrugged her narrow shoulders, a corner of her mouth quirked up, and there was that spark of mischief again. "Sure."

"Let's do it." Cole led her in the direction that Mack had gone. Beyond the barn, the sun sank closer to the horizon and the sky swirled with brilliant orange and pink. "Our timing is just right."

Liza stopped abruptly and faced him, wide-eyed. "What did you say?" Her voice was a little wobbly.

He hesitated before repeating himself, trying to figure out what had spooked her. "Our timing is just right. The sun is about to set."

She narrowed her eyes and searched his face, but he had no idea what she was looking for. Then she smiled sadly and, without a word, started walking again. Cole followed her closely, shaking his head in rhythm with the mesmerizing sway of her hips. They rounded the back of the barn just as Mack tossed a couple of blankets next to the hay bales stacked on a trailer he'd hitched to the truck.

Liza bit her bottom lip, grinning a little. "We're going on a hayride?"

"Please don't say you're allergic to hay," Cole teased. "Because then you'd have to drive, and I'd be stuck cuddling with Mack and watching the sunset."

Mack scrunched his nose. "Ain't no way that's happening."

Liza laughed, and Cole was struck by how much it changed her. She looked even prettier—carefree and sexy in a playful sort of way.

"I've never been on a hayride," she said.

"Really?"

She nodded. "I'm excited. Let's go."

The date Frank had planned couldn't have been simpler, but Liza was making it complicated for Cole. He'd never been out with a girl quite like her. Most of them were so predictable, so easy. But Liza had his head spinning like a nasty curveball. He wasn't sure if she liked him now or not, but she'd thought he was pretty cool years ago. The sun slid closer to the horizon, and he had the same sinking feeling in his stomach. He only had a few hours to convince her he was still the same guy who'd given her that autographed baseball.

· · ·

Liza settled in the hay near Cole, their legs stretched out in front of them, facing the sunset. Since this didn't qualify as a *real* date, she wasn't sure how close she should sit, or how close she could let herself get to him even so. Her best friend, Paige, would think she was crazy not to be on his lap by now, and Liza understood why. They could make a Cole Collins calendar to last for the next century and never run out of hot pictures of him. And Liza noticed the details—the way his shirt tightened perfectly across his muscular shoulders, how his blond hair flipped up a little in the back at the base of his collar, the way his long fingers had caressed that baseball. She didn't remember noticing things like that when they'd been teenagers. Cole simply being Cole had been enough to captivate her. But now, every little nuance had her full attention.

Mack pulled the truck and trailer onto a meandering dirt road that led away from the barn, heading east.

"This farm is like something out of a storybook," she said.

"Right? With a road special-made for sunset hayrides." Cole tipped his head back and gazed at the kaleidoscope sky, looking relaxed.

She took a deep breath herself, catching the heady scent of his cologne—definitely one of those with *bleu* in its name. She had no idea how a man could smell like a color, but blue was her favorite, and that's what Cole smelled like. Her heart skipped a beat faster, and she shifted just a little closer to him.

"Who owns this place?"

He narrowed his eyes, as if he were trying to think of a name. "A friend of Mack's."

"It was nice of them to let us come here." She and Cole had each grabbed a beer for the ride, and Liza sipped hers.

He raised his eyebrows playfully. "They're big Nats fans."

"Of course you have to go and ruin it for me." She grinned. "Deep down, they probably secretly like the Orioles, too."

"Um, no," he said with an impish gleam in his eyes. "They secretly do not."

"Ouch. Glad I came in disguise."

"I'm thinking that was a smart play." He smiled and ran his tongue across his bottom lip. Liza's insides went tingly. That was one mannerism of his she did remember—fondly. "I'm pretty sure the No Trespassing sign posted at the entrance was meant for Orioles fans."

"It was not!"

"Betcha."

Liza rolled her eyes. "Still, I'd love to live on a farm like this." She nudged him with her elbow and came up against taut muscle. "Where all sorts of fans would be welcome."

"You would?" He sounded surprised.

"Welcome all sorts of fans?" she teased. "Sure. I'd be an equal opportunity entertainer."

He shook his head, his lips curving up at the corners. "I just wouldn't have guessed you'd even think about living on a farm like this. That condo building of yours is very—what is it they call it?—cosmopolitan."

"It was kind of a convenience purchase," she said. Wes had preferred the city, but she had talked him into moving to suburbia someday, although someplace rural would've been ideal. But the two of them had never gotten the chance to live together at all. Her heart hurt just thinking about it. "I had…other plans that didn't work out, and I needed a change. My condo *is* cosmopolitan, but it's convenient to work, safe, peaceful." She shrugged. "But a place like this was my dream."

Cole shook his head. "Was?"

Liza's stomach clenched. She didn't want to tell him about Wes, so she shrugged casually. "I guess there's still time, isn't there?"

The sun sank lower, casting a pink hue across the landscape. Mesmerized by light and color, she and Cole watched the sunset in silence as the trailer dipped and swayed along the road, the air becoming cooler as the day turned to twilight. Just as the sun disappeared, as if on cue, Mack stopped the truck.

"We're here," Cole said, excitement in his voice. He stood and helped Liza up. It took a second for her to get her feet under her, then she and Cole jumped off the trailer.

"This is amazing," she said the moment she got a glimpse of their surroundings. They'd been facing backward during their hayride, so she had no idea they'd reached a large pond. A wooden dock stretched out from the shore, a small motorboat tethered to the end. White party lights were strung from pylon to pylon, waist-high along the dock. Just onshore was a fire pit—with logs and kindling set Boy-Scout perfect, just waiting for a match—with two red Adirondack chairs facing the fire and the pond. The chairs were decked out with navy blue cushions on the seat and back—the back ones embroidered with the white curly W that was the Nationals' logo.

"You weren't kidding about these people being fans," Liza said. "All the way down to their chair cushions."

Cole gave her an I-told-you-so nod, and Mack got busy off-loading a cooler and a big, old-fashioned picnic basket from the truck. Liza walked toward the dock, taking it all in.

In the background, Mack said to Cole, "Just give me a buzz when you're ready to head home. And you two kids enjoy yourselves."

"Thanks, Mack," Liza called.

Mack waved, started the truck, and drove off. The taillights and the rumble of the engine faded into the dusk, leaving her alone with Cole. She had a fleeting thought about her challenging fund-raising goal at BADD and wondered how much money she could raise toward it if she sold this time to women in five-minute increments.

Amid a flutter of nerves, she headed back up toward the fire pit, wishing she'd read the charity-auction-date-with-a-playboy handbook for some pointers on how she was supposed to act.

"You hungry?" he asked.

No matter what, she could always find her appetite. "Definitely," she said. "What's on the menu?"

• • •

"No chef tonight," Cole said. "Just you and me and two long sticks." He pulled his Swiss Army knife from his pocket and grabbed one of the two sweet-gum sticks that were propped against a chair. With a quick and easy motion, he stripped the bark off the end and started whittling it into a wicked point.

"What are we cooking?"

"I figured we'd go super-gourmet and roast some hot dogs."

She gave him a wide smile that made him feel as though he'd hit a home run. "My favorite."

"Seriously?" He was surprised how happy it made him to see her so pleased. Narrowing his eyes, he examined his handiwork on the first stick.

"Absolutely." She picked up the second stick and handed it to him, then took the first one and propped it by the chair. "Baseball, hot dogs…I'm sort of lukewarm on the apple pie."

"What?" He scrunched his face. "That's un-American."

"No, I mean it's okay once in a while, but between you and me…" She clutched his arm, stood on her tiptoes, and whispered in his ear, "I've been tempted by other flavors."

The wisp of her breath in his ear sent warmth surging through him. "You know what they say about variety," he teased.

"My best friend Paige owns a pie shop—well, a bakery—so I get to try some really good ones."

"No one makes 'em like my grandma."

"Aw. I remember you saying she made pies from the wild blackberries you picked. Is she still around?" Liza asked tentatively.

Cole's heart hitched. Why had he even mentioned his grandma, and how had Liza even remembered what he'd told her about the blackberries? He stopped whittling and shook his head. "No. And I really miss her. But I had her for twenty-one years. She pretty much raised me…but you already knew that."

Liza looked serious and sad, as if hearing about his loss had really affected her. "I'm so sorry." She gazed out over the pond for a long moment. "It's so hard to lose the people you love." She shrugged slowly, the gesture somehow making her slim shoulders look heavy. "When it comes down to it, there are so few people who truly know us." Her eyes glistened in the firelight. "When one of them goes, you can never replace them."

A log shifted in the fire, spitting sparks into the air. Liza smiled wanly, then turned and opened the picnic basket, making herself busy. He finished up his whittling job, trying to get his bearings. She had totally switched up the game on him. Considering the number of women he'd dated, he thought he'd seen everything. But she was showing him something completely different, and he didn't quite know how to handle it.

Liza got out all the fixings for the hot dogs, and he grabbed the foil-wrapped buns, nestling them near the fire where they'd get warm. His stomach growled loudly. He quickly flattened his hand across it and glanced at Liza.

"We need to get you fed," she said, reminding him of another thing his grandma used to say.

Cole handed her a stick, blond for several inches on the end and finely pointed, if he did say so himself. "Believe me, this upscale dinner will be worth the wait." He tore open the packet of hot dogs and presented them to her. "First course."

She pinched a hot dog between her index finger and thumb, pulled it out of the packet, and stabbed it straight through the middle. It drooped on both ends, and she gave it a forlorn look that made him laugh.

He raised his eyebrows. "I guess it's safe to say you weren't a Girl Scout."

She shook her head, laughing at herself—another thing he liked about her.

"You might not want to cook it that way." He took out another hot dog, skewered it in the end and through its center, and traded sticks with her. "You don't want to lose your wiener in the fire."

She grinned and reoriented the hot dog on his stick.

Satisfied, she said, "Let's cook, now that we've got our wieners straight."

He busted out laughing again.

They sat on the edges of the chairs, hot dogs roasting in the flames. Darkness had fallen, crickets chirped, and stars sparkled in the sky. Everything seemed idyllic, including Cole's growing desire to touch her. And despite feeling guilty about Frank's plan, he had to move things along if it was going to work. He reached over and took her hand, but moments after he touched her, she jerked it away, yanking her stick from the flames and jumping to her feet. "My hot dog's on fire!"

She waved it in the air until the flames died and left the charred and blistered hot dog sizzling and popping. Looking defeated, she sank onto the arm of the chair. "Did I mention I'm not much of a cook?"

Cole couldn't help but smile. "You didn't really have to."

She swatted his arm playfully. "What you see is what you get."

Cole couldn't hope for much more. Even so, he wondered whether he would still be holding her hand if her hot dog hadn't burst into flames. He switched sticks with her and loaded his up again.

They sipped beer and ate hot dogs and chips, kicked back in their chairs. The conversation was easy, and mostly about baseball. Cole was amazed how much she knew about the game, even considering her pedigree. Most of the women he dated didn't know the difference between an ERA and an RBI, but Liza could quote stats for every one of the Orioles and a lot of the Nats, too — including his. He was feeling kind of hopeful after that. Hopeful enough to celebrate with s'mores.

"Better job with the marshmallows," he said as she pulled them away from the flames, expertly browned. "No extinguisher required." He grinned.

"I'm teachable," she said as they stacked up their s'mores. She took an enthusiastic bite, and oozing chocolate and melted marshmallow squished out at the corner of her mouth. Staring at the fire, she slowly licked her lips, lingering where the chocolate and marshmallow had been. The firelight lit her face and danced in her eyes. Cole watched intently, shifting in his seat as pressure built inside him.

The girl was all over the ballpark, but he definitely wanted to kiss her.

Chapter Four

The fire burned low, and Liza stared at the nearly full moon that had risen in the sky. Relaxed in her chair—despite the Nationals cushion—she glanced at Cole. After they'd finished eating, he had casually reached for her hand and hadn't let go since. Not that she wanted him to. He kept skimming his fingers slowly across hers and tracing circles in her palm. No doubt he could seduce a woman with that technique alone. "You have a game tomorrow, right?" she asked.

He smiled, his eyes dancing with excitement. "One step closer to the division title, then the pennant, then the World Series."

"Don't get too far ahead of yourself, mister," she teased. "Other teams have that same strategy in mind."

"It's going to happen, so I'll start consoling you now." He leaned forward in his chair and faced her, looking twelve kinds of sexy by the fire. She tensed, thinking he was going to make a move, which both thrilled and terrified her. It had been so long, and she wasn't sure she was ready. But he made a goofy face instead and cocked his head. "Poor Liza," he said, doing a pretty good imitation of Eeyore.

She laughed and shook her head. "We'll see. One game at a time. The Os will be in the Series." She tipped up her chin proudly. "Maybe I'll see you there."

She realized she was in a perfect position for him to kiss her, and her heart thumped so hard she was afraid he might hear it. Cole gazed at her a moment with a look she couldn't read and squeezed her hand tightly. "This has been fun." She stared at his perfect mouth and thought about how incredible it would feel to have those lip on hers—just as she had when she was sixteen. "But it's getting kind of late. Guess I'd better call Mack."

Her heart sank with disappointment and relief—if that were even possible. He probably had no idea what was appropriate to do on a charity auction date, either. "Good idea."

They leisurely packed their gear. Mack got there quickly, and Liza wondered where he'd been all this time. She hated to think he'd been parked down near the barn, hanging out by himself, just waiting for them to call. But he seemed to be in good spirits when he arrived.

She and Cole climbed onto the trailer and sat close in the sweet-smelling hay, and he casually tossed a blanket over their legs. Mack started the truck and they headed back toward the barn.

"The s'mores were my favorite," Liza said, more bummed than she thought she'd be that their date was nearly over.

"I don't know," he said. "I thought the hot dogs were pretty good. At least your second one was. Not even the vultures would eat that first one."

"I told you I'm not much of a cook." She propped her elbow on the hay bale next to her. "But I can make a mean tiki torch with a flaming hot dog on a stick. Martha Stewart would have to give me some credit for that. I mean, as hard as it is to imagine, isn't there something you're just not good at?"

"Hmm." He rubbed his forehead. "No." He grinned and she nudged him with her elbow.

"Aw, come on. You're good at *everything*?"

He nodded. "And I have specialties."

Oh my… She was sure he did.

"He can't sing," Mack shouted from inside the truck. His windows were down, but Liza had no idea he could hear them.

"You can't sing?" she asked teasingly.

"I can," he said, "just not very well."

"Nice to know you aren't totally perfect." She nodded. "And a good thing you wanted to be a baseball player instead of a rock star, huh?"

"Thanks, Mack," Cole yelled playfully.

"Anytime."

Liza had calmed down little by little since Cole had casually blindsided her with Wes's special words…*just right*. But after that, the evening *had* been just right, with the hayride and the sunset and dinner by the campfire under the stars. There was still some of that teenage guy she'd had a crush on under Cole's All-Star persona. She'd think a little differently of him next time she saw him on *E!*.

The truck took the last bend before the barn, then came to an abrupt stop. Mack got out and hurried around to the side of the trailer. "Looks like we've got company."

Cole lowered his eyebrows and glanced at Liza, then got up and joined Mack, both of them looking toward the barn. She stood in the trailer and got a view over the cab of the truck. Artificial light radiated from the far side of the barn, illuminating the rear of a television news van and several other vehicles.

"Reporters," Cole said flatly.

Liza's stomach clenched. "All the way out here?" She was

amazed they'd be interested in Cole's date with *her*. "Want to try another way out?" Cole asked Mack.

The crease between Mack's eyes deepened and he shook his head. "Not a good idea to go headin' down some makeshift road without a little daylight. It'd be like runnin' down a rabbit hole."

"We could wait them out," Cole said. "But they've spotted our headlights by now. I'm sorry, Liza." He shifted his gaze between her and Mack.

"It's not your fault," she said anxiously. She wasn't big on being in front of a camera.

Cole leaped up onto the trailer, went to Liza, and gently put his hand on her shoulder. He was all tense muscle and tousled hair, and he still smelled smoky from the fire. "I didn't want a bunch of reporters spoiling our date. I'd hoped to get some privacy for a change."

"It won't be spoiled," she said. Nothing could ruin the evening they'd had.

Cole nudged her shoulder and gave her a sidelong glance, looking perfect in the moonlight.

"So you're up for a photo shoot?" He rubbed his hands together, seeming a little nervous himself.

She figured they might get some positive press for BADD, and that would be good. Maybe someone would see a news clip about the auction date and decide they wanted to donate. Heck, maybe she could make a pitch—she was nearly that desperate to find a way to meet her fund-raising goal. She shrugged and gave Cole a half smile. "Sure."

"No way around it except to face 'em," Mack said as he got back in the truck.

She and Cole sat on top of a hay bale and pulled the blanket over their knees. The trailer swayed and bounced over the last bit of dirt road, Cole steadying Liza with his arm around her. He turned toward her, pulled her close, tenderly kissed her on the cheek, and spoke softly in her ear. "Thanks for being such a good sport about this." Feathery sensations fluttered through her, and she shivered.

"It'll be fine," she said, believing that it would.

Mack pulled the truck and trailer alongside the barn. Before Liza and Cole had time to move, several reporters, cameramen, and photographers crowded behind the trailer. Liza squinted against the flash and glare of the lights. A middle-aged female reporter—dressed in a business suit and looking too city for an assignment on a farm—took the lead with questions. "Cole," she said, as if she knew him personally, "isn't this the date you donated to raise money for the BADD Athletes Foundation?"

"Yes," he said. "It's a good cause. I hope more people will learn about the important work BADD is doing to keep athletes drug-free." He glanced at Liza. The corners of his mouth turned up slightly, and his eyes sparkled with the reflection of lights from the cameras. "But I'm the one who benefited here. Look who I got to spend an evening with."

Liza swallowed hard, thinking it was awesome that he seemed proud to be with her, and he'd pretty much made her donation pitch, too. She probably had a silly-looking grin on her face, but she couldn't help it.

The reporter piped up again. "I have it from a reliable source that you might be settling down with Miss Sutherland."

Liza's grin flattened, and her heart raced double-time. What *reliable* source would've told the reporter that?

"Any truth to that rumor?" the reporter asked. "Inquiring women want to know." Several of the photographers chuckled.

Liza couldn't believe they even had to ask. Cole wasn't settling down—he probably never would, and certainly not with her. She turned to him, hoping he had a clever answer.

He glanced at her with a glint in his eyes, then turned back to the reporters. "Settling down is looking like a pretty good idea."

Liza's stomach clenched. *What?*

"Should we expect a proposal soon?" another reporter asked. "I'd love to be there for an exclusive on that."

The flash of a camera highlighted the mischief in his eyes, and a wisp of a sexy smile played across his lips. "It'll probably go something like this," he said with a drawl. He faced Liza, skimmed his fingertips along her jawline, and guided her head until she met his gaze.

Her mind swirled with confusion. All she could think was, *Please don't kiss me here…now!* She frantically wondered how to react to him in front of these people—in front of everyone, for that matter. Any stupid move she made would be captured on video and posted on YouTube forever.

He leaned closer, and Liza braced herself.

"Will you marry me, darlin'?" he asked.

Liza's heart lurched. Stunned speechless, she blinked several times, her pulse thrumming in her ears. Cole tipped his head and whispered in her ear, "Just smile." His warm breath sent another shiver through her, and she smiled with sheer bewilderment. He leaned back and tugged playfully on a lock of her hair, a crooked, coy grin on his face.

After a beat, he faced the reporters and winked as the cameras clicked and whirred. "That's as close to an exclusive as I can give you."

• • •

Cole was relieved that Liza had remained tight-lipped. He'd gotten caught up in the moment, always eager to tease the reporters. Mack had immediately sensed trouble and pulled the truck and trailer away from them. They continued calling out questions as Cole and Liza disappeared up the road and out of view. The reporters had cleared out from the farm pretty fast after that. Now he, Cole, and Liza weren't far behind them, back in the truck and headed to Baltimore.

"That was...pretty awkward," Liza said, then bit her bottom lip. "I wasn't expecting something like that to happen." Cole should've guessed that Frank would send the media, but his strategy might've backfired. Things had been going pretty well between him and Liza up until then, and he'd been feeling pretty confident about getting a second date. After that, they'd be off and running with their so-called romance.

But Frank had sent the press in way too soon, and Cole had tried to wing it. Now that he'd teased the reporters into thinking he wanted to settle down with Liza, he needed her to play the part. Deep down, he *wanted* her to play the part. Besides, if he showed up with another girl anytime soon and said the same thing, he'd ruin his credibility and the Nats would catch on to him.

Cole flexed his shoulders, trying to ease his tension. He'd faced some of the toughest pitchers in major league baseball and hadn't felt as knotted up as he did right now. He looked at her sheepishly. "I'm sorry. I don't mind the sports reporters, but the others who are obsessed with my personal life get *too* personal. They claim they have 'insider information' that mostly comes from their imagination, so it's tiring dealing with that all the time." He shrugged. "Sometimes it's so ridiculous I just have to go along and make fun of it. As if I'd want any of them around when I did something as personal as propose."

He watched her face in the darkness, looking for signs that she understood, but it was hard to tell with the changing light and shadows.

After a while, she nodded. "I can understand how you feel

about the reporters. They'd probably get to me after a while, too. Asking if you were settling down *was* kind of ridiculous considering…"

Cole stiffened. "Considering what?" He knew what she meant, but he wanted to hear her answer just the same.

"That you're a player." Man, she sure got straight to the point.

He sucked in a deep breath. "I can't deny that." He couldn't say much more without revealing more to her than he wanted to.

"There's nothing wrong with it if it works for you," she said, "especially since you're up-front about it. But I guess I'm a little more…traditional."

Cole winced. He caught Mack's eye in the rearview mirror. Just a glance told him Mack didn't envy his position but that he was there for him, as he had been for years. He'd seen and heard a lot, and he knew a lot of secrets, but he'd never betrayed Cole's confidence.

"Since that's your reputation," she said, "none of what you did back there made sense."

Cole didn't like where this was going, and he hated that they'd lost that easy feeling they'd had going after dinner back at the farm. "I can see how you'd be confused," he said. "But believe it or not, settling down is looking better to me all the time."

She gave him a small smile. "Then I hope you find someone to settle down with, if that's what you really want. But I just got caught in the middle of something that I'm not even involved in. Who knows what those reporters are going to do with that news, whether it's true or not."

Cole furrowed his brow. Plan or no plan, he really wanted to make things right with her.

He looked out the window and got his bearings. They

were just minutes from Liza's condo, and soon she would be gone. Whatever he was going to do to save this situation, he had to do it now.

"I really screwed up." He rested his head in his hand for a second, then dragged his fingers down his face. "It wasn't the smartest move I've ever made back there." He risked taking her hand and she didn't pull away. It occurred to him that this might be the last chance he'd have to touch her, and he started to panic a little, surprising himself. "I really had fun tonight, and I'd like to go out with you again. Maybe we can pick up where we left off before—" He tipped his head back in the direction of the farm. "All that." He brought her hand to his mouth and lightly kissed her palm.

She blinked several times, then stared at him for a long moment. He just might give his Gold Glove award to know what she was thinking.

"Come to my game tomorrow," he said, unable to stand her silence any longer. "I'll leave tickets for you at Will Call—and we'll go out afterward."

Liza furrowed her brow and rubbed her glossy lips together slowly, reminding him how much he wanted to kiss her.

She shook her head just as Mack pulled the truck in front of her building and stopped. "Thank you for tonight. It was good to catch up with you after all this time." She squeezed his hand and released it. "But I won't be there tomorrow."

She might as well have punched him in the gut. Admittedly, he'd been a *little* worried, but her calm attitude about the media mess had him fooled into thinking she'd say yes to another date. Cole's stomach clenched. Frank was going to kill him, but only after he beat *himself* up over what he had done.

Liza didn't waste any time waiting for him to open her

door, and within seconds she was out of the truck.

"It was nice to meet you, Mack," she said, then gently closed the door.

Cole got out quickly, but she hurried inside the building and disappeared from view. He stood in her wake for a little while, trying to get his head around what had just happened.

Mack rolled down his window. "You goin' after her?"

Cole raked his hand through his hair and pulled at the back of it until it hurt. "Not tonight." He got in the front seat, more comfortable riding shotgun than staring at the back of Mack's prickly gray head all the way home. "That was worse than a strikeout."

Mack nodded. "You could say that." He put the truck in gear and headed toward DC. Cole pulled out his phone and speed-dialed Frank.

"Evenin', Cole," Frank answered, sounding wide-awake even though it was past midnight. "How'd it go, son?"

Cole took a deep breath and exhaled loudly. "I think we're gonna need a plan B."

Chapter Five

Liza pushed herself harder on her Saturday morning run, letting a little angst over her job fuel her energy and distract her from thinking about last night's date with Cole—which was pretty much all she'd thought about since. Everyone had such high hopes for it, and she had to admit she'd had a little hope too, although she wasn't sure for what. Certainly not for that crazy proposal stunt Cole had pulled.

Think about work… Think about work… She kept a steady pace alongside Baltimore's Inner Harbor, excited about the plans she was making for the BADD camps next year. She loved that part of her job. But the foundation was small and depended on "collective development," a fancy way of saying that most of the management-level employees had to meet an annual fund-raising goal. And Liza had missed hers by several thousand dollars last year.

The economy wasn't rosy, and her donors had been maxed out. She'd gotten dinged in her performance appraisal despite the outstanding job she did otherwise. When her mom found out Liza had come up short on her goal and not asked for money, things had gotten pretty tense. But Liza would rather fail on her own than be propped up by her parents. And failure was likely to happen, since it was already September, and she was nowhere near on target for this year's goal.

She did pretty well recruiting the pro players to teach at the camps, and that probably counted for something. But raising money? Outside of the donors she already had, who could she ask that her parents hadn't hit up already?

At the end of her fourth mile, Liza slowed to a walk, shifting her thoughts from work to Wes. Breathing hard, she swept her hand across her sweaty forehead and wiped it on her shirt. Wes would be proud that she now could run four miles without nearly passing out. They'd been training before he died, hoping to run a half marathon together someday. She'd done a couple of 5Ks in memory of him, but she wasn't sure about ever finishing a half marathon. A welcome cool breeze blew in from the harbor, smelling briny and carrying a hint of autumn. Another season without him.

She was amazed how life had gone on, as if the world hadn't noticed he was missing. But she noticed every day. When she heard something funny that she knew would make him laugh. When she got a text, and for a blissful moment thought it might be from him. When she went to bed at night and longed to have him there beside her…

She found an empty bench near the harbor and slumped down on one end of it, still a little out of breath. The bench was cool against the backs of her legs, but the sun warmed her face and danced over the harbor's wavering surface. She took a slug of water from the bottle she'd brought along as several pigeons clustered around, hoping to get fed.

Her thoughts circled back to Cole again. He'd been way more down-to-earth than she'd expected him to be, and even sexier than she'd imagined. She shivered, recalling the whisper of his breath in her ear, the touch of his perfect lips to her palm. Those could've been playboy moves, but the lost look in his eyes when he talked about his grandma had been totally real. Even so, he'd taken things too far with his ruse to the reporters. But he had seemed genuinely sorry, and he'd even sent her a tweet last night after he'd left.

Cole Collins @ColeCollins
@LizaSutherland No threat of fiery hot dogs at Nats park. Leaving tix at Will Call. Surprise date after the game? #youwillneverguess

He hadn't given up, and it made her happy for him to publicly ask her on a real date, even though it was hard to believe. Yet she hadn't responded. She wasn't up for the drama—at least that's what she told herself. Now she could stop worrying about how the date would go and get back to her life. Baseball games, BADD camps, Wes…

A large, middle-aged man dressed in a red wind shirt ambled over and sat at the other end of the bench. She glanced at him quickly and nodded. He looked like an average weekend-morning bench-sitter with a newspaper tucked under his arm and a venti Starbucks cup that looked like a tall in his hand. His hairline was quickly receding from a heavy-featured face. She vaguely recognized him, but she couldn't figure from where. Ex-athlete maybe, from back in her dad's era?

"Good morning, Miss Sutherland," he said pleasantly.

So she must have met him before. Lots of people knew of her because of her parents and because of her job. People she might not recognize right away, if at all.

"Have we met?" she asked.

"Frank Price." He laid the newspaper on the bench and offered one of his beefy hands.

The legendary sports agent? No wonder he looked familiar. He represented at least one Oriole player that Liza knew of, and lots of other big-name athletes.

"I know your folks," he said, "and I've seen you around with them. But I don't believe I've had the pleasure of meetin' you."

She shook his hand, thinking it was a cool coincidence that he'd sat with her. Things really were going pretty well today. "Nice to meet you, Mr. Price," she said, feeling self-conscious in her Lycra shorts and sweaty Under Armour tee.

"Call me Frank," he said.

"Are you in Baltimore on business?"

"You could say that. I'm workin' on a pretty important deal."

Liza raised her eyebrows. "That's exciting. At least to me." She shrugged. "Guess it's everyday stuff for you."

"Not this deal. It's one-of-a-kind." He shifted on the bench and faced her. "And it involves you."

Me? She scrunched her face. "I don't understand."

"I'm Cole Collins's agent…"

Liza's stomach sank, then fluttered.

"…and I liked the idea that you two got together on that date last night."

She crossed her arms, suddenly chilly and breaking out in goose bumps.

Frank opened the newspaper to a specific page, folded it into a rectangle, and handed it to her. It was the sports section of today's *Washington Post*, featuring a full-color photo of her and Cole, sitting close on a hay bale, just after he'd fake-proposed and asked her to smile. He was tugging on a lock of her hair, smiling too, and they looked completely into each other. The headline read, "Practice Proposal: All-Star Collins Serious about More Than Baseball."

Liza's pulse thrummed in her temples, and her stomach went a little queasy. If she had seen the picture of Cole and another girl, she would've believed the headline, no question. But she was that girl. She shook her head and handed the newspaper back to Frank. "You must know he wasn't serious."

"Oh, I wouldn't say that." He set the paper on the bench between them and gazed at the photo. "You two look pretty cozy to me."

"He was joking around with the reporters…and me."

"He mighta been kiddin' about the proposal, but he still thinks you're special." Frank seemed pretty sure of himself. "You had him reelin' when you turned him down for another date."

Liza smiled skeptically. "He seems to think lots of girls are special."

Frank shook his head and frowned. "The boy has a reputation when it comes to the ladies, and I can see why that might scare you off. But I've gotten to know him pretty well over the years, and I can tell you this for sure: he's just looking for something meaningful in all the wrong places. You're not just any girl to him. You two had a connection back when you were kids, and he hoped there was still something there."

Really?

He *had* officially asked her out. Excitement welled inside her at the thought of seeing him again. But could she do that to Wes? She'd been coaxed into going on the auction date, and that had eased some of her guilt. Going on a real date would be harder to justify.

"I was happy to see him again," she said. "But things have changed a lot since we were teenagers."

Frank furrowed his forehead, his thick eyebrows shading his eyes. "I understand you've had a challenging go of it, with your fiancé passing and all, so I could see why you might hesitate to take up with Cole."

She swallowed hard. Frank had no idea. "So Cole knows about Wes?"

"No. I figured it wasn't my place to tell him."

Liza was thankful for that. Imagine how much more complicated things might've been if pity was thrown into the mix last night. She glanced down at the picture of her and Cole. The camera might fool her into thinking he really did like her, especially considering Frank's claims. If Wes hadn't been in her life, she might've picked right up with that crush she'd had on Cole, despite his reputation. But Wes *had* been in her life, and left her. He hadn't hurt her intentionally, but the pain was just as real. Even if she could get past her grief, she wasn't about to take a chance on a guy like Cole.

"I hear he invited you to his game today," Frank said. "You should go. Then you two can get together again and see what happens."

Liza watched a cargo ship sail slowly across the hazy horizon. "It was nice of you to come, and it was very cool to meet you." She shrugged. "Cole's a good guy, and I'm sure he has a bright future...but it won't be with me."

Frank nodded. "I think it just might."

Jeez. She'd politely told the guy no, so he should politely give up.

"I've got a deal for you," he said.

Liza sighed. "I'm not interested in a deal—whatever that means."

Frank propped his elbows on his knees and rolled his coffee cup between his hands. "I understand you're pretty dedicated to BADD, and I really respect that. Cole does, too. You do a fine job with those camps for needy boys."

"Less fortunate," she said absently. It was starting to creep her out a little that he knew so much about her.

"I bet five hundred thousand dollars could pay for a lot of less fortunate boys to go to camp next year."

Her stomach swirled. She narrowed her eyes, wondering if she'd heard him right. "You want to donate a half-million dollars to BADD?" That would beat the crap out of her fund-raising goals from now until forever. She imagined how shocked her coworkers would be when she announced she'd raised a cool half-mil—on her own.

"Not so fast. I said a deal, not a donation."

No wonder so many athletes wanted him for their agent. Now that he had her dreaming about landing a donation like that, he was going to tell her exactly what she had to do to get it. *And it's going to involve Cole.* She gulped down some water and braced herself. "What's the deal?"

"It's really simple. It would make Cole happy if you'd give him a chance. I don't like to interfere, but when Cole is happy, he plays some mean baseball. When he's not…well, things can get ugly." Frank gazed out over the harbor, looking pensive. "This is an important time for him and the Nationals. It's in my best interest to keep him squared away. Sure, it's about business for me, but it's more than that." He picked up the newspaper. "I really like the kid. I know he was foolin' around with those reporters, but it'd be nice to see him look that happy all the time."

She was touched by Frank's attachment to Cole, even though he stood to gain from his player's success. At least he'd been up-front about it. "So if I give Cole a chance, you'll donate a half-million dollars to BADD?"

"I wouldn't put it that way." He gave her a fatherly smile. "I want you to give yourself a chance, too. A couple months is all I'm asking. Go out with Cole. Get to know him. Have a good time. You're gonna fall for him, I'm sure. He's already falling for you."

"If he is," Liza said, "it happened pretty fast. One charity-auction date and a phony headline in a newspaper aren't enough to convince me."

"Hear me out, now. These are the terms." Now Frank was really starting to sound like an agent. "Date Cole for two months, and be yourself. No shenanigans. You're gonna be totally smitten with him again. If you're not, I'll donate five hundred thousand dollars to BADD."

Liza shook her head. Something like this had happened in a romance novel she'd read, and it was too far-fetched to believe it was happening to her, in real life. "I don't think I'm going to be smitten with Cole." *Am I?* "Didn't I make that clear?"

He raised his eyebrows, his lips turned up at the corners. "Then it's easy money for BADD."

She stalled by retying the loose lace of her running shoe. After what seemed like a long time but was probably only seconds, she said, "I don't think I can do that."

He nodded. "Then you need to think some more."

This guy doesn't give up.

Surprised and a little disturbed that she was giving his offer further thought, she considered the pros and cons. Two months hanging out with Cole. Her heart beat a little faster. How bad could that be? He was interesting to talk to about baseball, and incredibly easy to look at. *And super sexy, too.* Besides, he was busy playing right now, and he'd be traveling a lot—especially if the Nationals made the playoffs. She started wishing they would.

There was no risk of falling for him anyway, because she had her memories of Wes.

But people will think I've forgotten him.

The corners of the newspaper fluttered in the breeze, drawing her gaze to the picture of her and Cole in the

Washington Post. The word was out. Even before the picture and the article showed up in the paper, there were tweets about their date—from BADD, and Paige, and others. Although it wasn't true, it already looked like she'd moved on. Her heart knew better, and that's what mattered. *Right?* If she did this, she'd be doing it for BADD, and for those boys who dreamed of playing college baseball and just needed a chance.

"I thought you were a shrewd dealmaker," she said. "But now I'm not so sure."

Frank looked amused. "Why's that?"

"You can't negotiate people's emotions."

He nodded. "Unless you're pretty sure—and I am."

"What about Cole?"

"Don't tell him," he said sternly. "This stays between you and me."

"That's not what I meant." She couldn't believe what she was about to say. "What if he really does fall for me?" *Could I resist him then?* And if she could, she certainly didn't want to hurt him, as far-fetched as the possibility might be.

"Then you'll be one lucky lady." His tone told her that negotiations were closed.

He pulled an envelope from between the pages of the newspaper and handed it to her. "Here it is in black and white."

She opened the envelope and pulled out two identical official-looking documents detailing Frank's offer.

> *I, Liza Sutherland, agree to:*
> *—Date Cole Collins through the end of the current baseball season, which includes attending Nationals games when asked, and functions when invited.*
> *—Be myself. No games or manipulation.*
> *—Keep this arrangement confidential.*

If I adhere to the aforementioned and do not fall in love with Cole Collins, Frank Price will immediately donate $500,000 via Liza Sutherland to the BADD Athletes Foundation.

Frank had signed both copies, and there was a space for her to sign as well, with her name typed beneath it.

Liza grimaced and folded the papers. "BADD really needs that money, but I can't do something sleazy like this to get it."

Frank raised one eyebrow. "It's not sleazy to raise money for a charity that'll send poor kids to camp. Did you think it was sleazy for Cole to donate a date to BADD's auction? There's really not much difference in that and what I'm asking you to do."

He kind of had a point. Even so, she felt like she needed a shower, and not just from being sweaty.

"I still can't do it," she said.

He gave her a wry smile. "Can you really afford not to?"

BADD could use the money, and she really did want to see Cole again…but she'd never admit that to Frank.

"It's really counterintuitive, though. I don't fall for Cole, and you donate the money to BADD."

"Sounds like you've got it figured out."

"I think I do." *Don't I?* She risked considering what would happen if she did fall for Cole—a long shot that no sane person would bet on. She'd end up empty-handed for BADD, which was no worse off than she was right now. But what about her heart?

"Then have we got a deal?" He reached in his pocket, pulled out a Montblanc pen, and handed it to her.

She pressed her eyes closed for a few seconds. Could she really say no? Her hands trembled a little as she unscrewed the cap from the pen and signed her name on the papers. She kept one for herself, put the other back in the envelope, and gave it to Frank along with his pen.

"Nice doing business with you." He smiled again, flashing lots of big, white teeth. "Now run in and get yourself dolled up." He tossed his coffee cup toward a nearby trash can, and it bounced off the rim and went in. "You've got a ball game to get to."

Chapter Six

Cole stepped into the on-deck circle and practiced his swing with a weight on his bat, keeping an eye on the action of the game. The Nationals needed this win against the Braves, and usually the first team that scored ended up winning. The game had been hitless through two and a half innings until the guys at the top of the lineup got a couple of knocks, and were now on first and third with one out. Momentum was going their way.

But the batter at the plate struck out. A fair number of Braves fans cheered and started that stupid tomahawk chop. Cole checked the pine tar on his bat, tapped the weight off onto the ground, and headed toward the batter's box. He tried not to let the crowd distract him during games, and he rarely looked up at the Diamond Club seats where players' friends and families sat.

Most of his friends were on the bases, in the dugout, or in the bullpen, anyway. And they were pretty much his family, too. Whether he looked or not, he could bank on Mack being up there in the Diamond Club seats, sometimes with his wife, Brenda, and often with Frank. He was always nervous when they were there and watching—it was a different kind of pressure. The eyes of a crowd of forty thousand didn't affect him like the eyes of the people he wanted to impress most.

But today he felt different—like he needed a boost of confidence since he'd blown it with Liza last night and botched Frank's plan. Deciding it was worth the pressure of Mack's gaze to get a little reassurance, Cole glanced up into the crowd and quickly located Mack. But the woman sitting next to him wasn't Brenda.

Liza?

The sun caught her hair just right, making it shimmer like dark copper. She stared straight at him and smiled. His heart hammered faster than the rhythm of his country-song walk-up music blaring in the background. He couldn't believe she'd changed her mind, but he wanted to run up into the stands and kiss her.

He was normally serious when he came to the plate, but this time he busted out a hell-yeah grin and winked at her. He took his stance and faced the pitcher, ready to knock that baseball out into the parking lot.

After two swinging strikes and one ball in the dirt, Cole got a fastball down the middle. He smacked it off the screws, tossed his bat, and sprinted for first, watching the ball ricochet off the right-field wall. As he rounded first and headed to second, his teammate scored, and the Nats took the lead.

Thanks to a hot redhead.

Standing on the bag at second, Cole took a deep breath and scanned the cheering crowd. He loved this team, and he loved these fans. This park was like his home. *Maybe Frank's plan is going to work.*

The prediction proved to be true—the first team that had scored had won. The Nats took it four-one, and were one step closer to the division title, just as Cole had told Liza they would be.

After the game, the celebrating, and the media interviews, he hit the clubhouse and showered in a hurry, anxious to get to Liza. One of his smart-ass teammates had bought thirty copies of today's *Washington Post* and plastered his and Liza's pictures in the shape of a big heart on the clubhouse wall. This morning, he could barely stand to look at the photo of them together—much less thirty of them—or good-naturedly take the teasing from the guys. But now he had hope, and his teammate's prank had quickly made the start of his fake relationship seem legit. He couldn't wait to see her again, so that made it *feel* kind of legit, too. He snapped a picture of the display and posted it on Twitter.

Cole Collins @ColeCollins
@LizaSutherland Nats clubhouse art. #epiccollage

Mack texted and told him he'd set Liza up in the Nats' family room, and Cole found her there. She sat on the edge of a leather armchair, her back to him, watching the *Nats Extra* postgame show on one of the flat screens. He hung in the background for a second while one of his teammates wrangled his toddler son, and his wife picked up toys.

Liza glanced behind her and caught sight of him. She stood, looking self-conscious *and pretty damn hot*, and gave him a shy smile.

Cole made his way past the chattering family, kind of nervous about how this was going to go, but confident he could pull it off now that he had a second chance.

She had her phone in hand and she tipped it toward him. "Nice tweet."

"You saw the newspaper, I guess."

She nodded, gazing at him with those pale green eyes.

"Sorry if it embarrassed you," he said sincerely.

"What do you mean 'if'?" She smiled brightly, and it calmed his nerves a little.

He rolled his eyes. "I'm glad you came," he said.

She smoothed her hands down the front of her faded jeans—they fit just as well or better than the black ones she'd worn last night—and tucked her hands into the pockets of her red zip-up hoodie. His gaze lingered on her snug, white V-neck tee. "And dressed like a Nats fan, too."

She blushed and gave her outfit a once-over. "Totally unintentional."

Again, he felt guilty about involving her in Frank's scheme. She had shown up *and* worn his team's colors. For some reason it reminded him of when she'd hung out and watched him at baseball camp.

"What made you change your mind?" he asked.

She lifted one shoulder. "The tweet you sent last night. The hot dog I had during the game was cooked perfectly." She grinned.

Cole flattened his hand against his chest, pretending to be wounded. "You mean it wasn't my irresistible charm and wit?"

She shook her head, looking coy. "But that *was* a pretty impressive double you hit."

He scrunched his nose. "I was aiming for the parking lot."

"You used to say that at baseball camp." She smiled. "Even though there wasn't a parking lot anywhere near the diamond."

"But there was a parking lot somewhere," he teased.

"I say take what good you can get, and next time make it better," she said. "Cheesy, huh?"

He kind of liked the way she came up with things that made him think. It was more than he could say for most of the girls he'd dated. "Sounds like something a coach would say."

"I got it from my dad—heard it about a million and twelve times when I was growing up." She cocked her head. "I'm surprised he didn't use it on you baseball-campers, too."

Cole tensed. "Maybe he did," he said flatly. "But that's a long time and a lot of coaches ago."

Liza winced at his tone, and Cole checked himself. She didn't seem to have a clue how her father had hurt him and shattered his confidence—something all those coaches had worked to undo. John Sutherland had become co-owner of the Orioles while Cole played at UNC. He had followed Cole's progress and built up his hopes of being drafted by the Orioles, assuring Cole there was a behind-the-scenes deal going on and that it was a sure thing. John and Sylvia had become surrogate parents to him over the years, and he was nearly as excited about being "officially" associated with them as he was about playing for the Orioles. But at the last minute, the Nationals had drafted him. Sutherland had given him some lame excuse about the draft being unpredictable, and claimed the Nationals had picked him up before the Orioles had the chance. Soon after that, John and Sylvia had drifted out of Cole's life, his confidence was shot, and his troubles in baseball began. But that was the last thing he planned to admit to Liza right now, if she hadn't figured it out herself.

He reached out and pulled one of the strings of her hoodie, just as he'd done last night with a lock of her hair. "Let's get out of here. I've got a surprise for you."

But Cole was the one who was surprised. He couldn't believe how happy he was that he had another date with her.

Chapter Seven

Liza and Cole walked hand-in-hand down the sidewalk along one of the quiet streets of tiny downtown Maple Creek, Maryland. The place always reminded her of Mayberry RFD, the town she'd seen in reruns of *The Andy Griffith Show* on TV Land. Maple Creek had lots of the same characters and a few modern touches. Mature trees flanked the road, and decorative banners of colorful fall leaves hung from the old-fashioned light posts.

A group of older ladies stood in front of the drugstore. Their heads turned in unison as Cole and Liza passed, their eyes wide behind their glasses. They didn't see many men under sixty in this town, so Cole was certainly an eye-catcher. Liza couldn't argue that.

He walked with a little swagger, his jeans set perfectly on his hips. As if he knew they were watching, he ran his hand through his hair—shiny in the afternoon sun and messy from the breeze. His plaid shirt rippled across his muscular shoulders as he raised his arm, and settled just tight enough across his pecs when he lowered it. Tall, rugged, and carefree, he looked like the walking inspiration for a sexy country song.

"Good heavens," one of the ladies said just loud enough for them to hear.

Liza rolled her eyes and shook her head. "Busted."

"What?" he asked playfully.

"You're shameless. Putting on a show like that for those old ladies. You're going to give them heart attacks."

"I didn't put on a show for them," he said, grinning guiltily.

But he had given Nats fans a show this afternoon. Liza had to admit she'd been impressed watching him play — so athletic and confident, with the crowd chanting his nickname, "Crush, Crush, Crush." The jumbotron scoreboard had flashed highlights of him making impossible plays with ease.

And I'm officially dating him.

The entire setup seemed surreal, but the guilt that was nagging her didn't. Was it okay to feel a little relaxed and kind of excited now that she knew where things were headed with Cole? *A half-million dollars for BADD.* She still felt kind of sleazy about what she was doing, but reassured herself that it was for a good cause. Just like Cole donating a date to the BADD auction...*right?*

They passed a small post office and a barbershop. "You're taking me to Sweet Bee's, aren't you?"

Liza never would've guessed he'd bring her to Maple Creek, and it tugged at her heart a little. She'd mentioned Paige's bakery last night, and he must have remembered. They stopped in front of the next storefront where a sunshine-yellow-and-pink striped awning shaded the doorway. The moment they stepped inside, they were enveloped by the sweet smell of cakes baking in the oven.

Paige came around from behind the glass display cases — filled with cookies and cakes and gorgeous pastries — and gave Liza a tight hug, her white apron dirty and her eyes dancing with mischief.

Liza worried what that might mean. "Cole, this is my best friend, Paige Ellerbee."

Paige was the size of a Polly Pocket doll with a face like a Disney princess, and the flair for drama to match it. She shifted her wide-eyed gaze between Cole and Liza. She'd hung on every word of the story Liza had told her about last night's date when she'd called on her way to the baseball game. But Liza had revised it a little. She'd left out the part about turning Cole down for another date, and the part about her deal with Frank. As far as Paige knew, all had gone smoothly, if not a bit strangely, for the two of them. She hadn't needed any more evidence than the picture she'd seen in a copy of the *Washington Post* that a customer left on a table.

Paige shook Cole's hand, looking way calmer than most people probably did when they met him. "Pleasure to meet you," she said, then flipped her blond ponytail. It had a streak of pink in it that matched the stripes in the awning. "Now I can mark you off of my ten-guys-I-gotta-meet-before-I-die list." She nodded, grinning.

Liza laughed. "I thought it was ten-guys-I-gotta—"

"Glad the Nats won today," Paige said quickly, and shot a no-you-didn't look at Liza.

"Nice to meet you, too," Cole said. "Thanks."

Liza could tell he didn't know what to make of Paige. She hadn't either, when she'd met her in third grade. Heading back from the bathroom, Liza had seen Paige standing alone outside her classroom, drawing smiley faces on the wall with a red Sharpie.

"Are you in trouble?" Liza had asked. "'Cause if you're not already, you're gonna be."

Paige had widened her golden-brown eyes, her blond hair falling in wisps from her ponytail. She'd looked like a Precious Moments figurine. "No I won't," she'd said politely. "This is art class."

"Everything's ready for you two." Paige gestured toward the door that led to the kitchen.

Liza glanced suspiciously between her and Cole. "What does that mean?"

Cole said, "You, Miss Tiki Torch Hot Dog, I'm-not-much-of-a-cook, are going to do some baking."

"You're kidding, right?" She would much rather do some eating.

"Nope." Paige's eyes glimmered.

Liza had no idea what they were talking about. Obviously the two of them had cooked up something before she and Cole got there. "Someone want to clue me in here?"

"Liza, you're like, all Orioles, all the time." Paige clutched Cole's biceps and raised her eyebrows at Liza. "And Cole is all Nationals, for sure. So I thought you two should settle this thing in the kitchen—you know, baseball pie wars or something."

"Baseball pie wars?" Liza asked.

Paige nodded. "Well, yeah. Because cake and cupcake competitions are so overdone. And I figured I'd have a real battle on my hands." She tipped her head toward Liza, looking exasperated. "But then you show up in that Nats outfit and I'd say the advantage goes to Cole." He played along, giving Paige a thumbs-up, and that only encouraged her. "I can count the times on my index finger that I've seen her wear something that wasn't black or orange."

"She's exaggerating," Liza said. *But not by a lot…*

"C'mon back." Paige led them into the kitchen, which gleamed with stainless steel. The place was so clean and organized that someone might wonder if all of the pastries and cakes up front had been delivered, and the kitchen was just for show. Liza knew better. After Wes died, she'd spent many days in here with Paige, trying to help but really only getting in the way. Yet Paige had never acted as if it bothered her—even when Liza botched recipes and left cookies in the oven way too long.

Since then, Liza had associated Sweet Bee's with her intense grief during the first months after she lost Wes. It had kept her away from Paige more than she wanted to admit, and still Paige had understood.

"So here's the setup," Paige said. "You two are going to create a team pie." She took another opportunity to grab Cole's biceps. "You'll make a Nationals pie, and Liza will make an Orioles pie. I'll help you come up with recipes, and then we'll see which one turns out best. Haven't you ever seen _Cupcake Wars_? It's like that, but with pie."

Liza was waiting for the punch line, and Cole looked as though he was trying not to laugh. "You're serious?" she asked, imagining the horror she might create considering she was chronically kitchen-challenged.

"What? Are you afraid of a little friendly competition?" Paige teased.

"No," Liza said quickly. "I just hate to embarrass him."

Cole laughed and smoothed his hand up and down her back. "I'm not too worried about that."

"Whatever," Liza said, enjoying the sturdy feel of his touch. "You'd be wise not to judge me based on one flaming wiener."

Paige raised one eyebrow. "I'm not sure I want to know what that means."

"Considering we're in your kitchen," Cole said, "and you're letting Liza cook, I'm guessing you don't." He flashed Liza a knowing smile, and her heart fluttered.

"I think I might," Paige teased. "But I'm willing to risk it. There's a fire extinguisher mounted right there on the wall.

Feel free to use it when you need to."

"Joke all you want," Liza said. "We'll see who's laughing later."

Paige glanced from Liza to Cole, and shrugged. "Game on." She checked her oversized watch. "We need to get moving. The judges will be here in two hours."

"Judges?" Liza knew she sounded freaked out. Just when she'd decided this could turn out to be fun with the three of them, Paige had gone and thrown in judges?

Paige nodded. "Handpicked and hungry for pie."

"Who?" Liza asked.

"You'll see. But we need to get to work now." Paige gestured to the right side of the kitchen. "Cole, you're over here. Liza's on the left. Backs to each other, so you can't check out the competition."

Liza felt a twinge of disappointment. Having her back to Cole made sense, but she'd kind of been looking forward to checking him out as often as she could while they were together. Frank's deal did offer some fine fringe benefits to offset some of her guilt.

Cole extended his hand to her, playing this whole thing up as if it were a reality TV show. Paige watched them closely as Liza shook his hand, his grip strong and sure. He gave her a crooked smile and sweetly said, "I'm going to crush you."

• • •

Cole wiped his forehead with the back of his hand. This baking stuff was *work*. When he was growing up, he'd helped his grandma in the kitchen, baking cookies or cobblers. But that had mostly involved licking the beaters and the bowl, then heading back outside to play baseball with his buddies. Now he understood just how much effort went into making a couple of pies.

But his wasn't an ordinary pie. It was a masterpiece.

He hurried to put the final touch on it—a curly-W logo in the center on top. He stepped back and admired his work, hoping the pie tasted as good as it looked. Paige had helped him decide on a recipe, but he'd done the rest himself. His grandma would be proud.

He couldn't wait to put his Nationals pie up against anything Liza had decided on for the Orioles. At first, he'd been skeptical of the whole idea, thinking of all the other things Frank could've arranged for them to do. But he was having fun joking with Paige and flirting with Liza. He got the feeling she might be starting to warm up to him the way she used to, and that pleased him more than he thought it would.

"Time's up, you two." Paige flitted into the kitchen like a sprite. "And everyone's here."

"Already?" Liza asked.

Cole had been so intent on making his pie and stealing glances at Liza that he hadn't paid attention to what had been going on out front.

"Go on and say hi," Paige said. "I'll bring the pies in a little bit."

Cole started to take off his chef's apron—now stained with red and blue—but Paige stopped him. "Leave it on. It'll give you some cred."

Cole met Liza near the door. He tried to get a look at her pie, but she'd blocked it from his view. He'd done the same thing.

"Feeling confident?" he taunted good-naturedly.

"You didn't smell anything burning, did you?"

"I figured that would be your grand finale—Orioles pie flambé." He grinned. "Smarter to set the pie on fire in front of the judges. It might get you the sympathy vote."

"Whatever it takes to beat you."

"You're not going to win."

She playfully tipped up her chin. "Wanna bet?"

Her offer shocked him. He was so sure he would win, and he was so sure she knew it. "All right." He couldn't keep the cocky smile off his face.

"If I win…" She bit her lip as she thought about her wager. Cole gazed appreciatively at her mouth, knowing exactly what his wager was going to be. "I want you to give me autographed baseball cards for the BADD camp kids."

It struck him how she'd picked something for others, instead of choosing something for herself. Cole remembered being a teenager headed to camp, carrying along his cherished John Sutherland card that he'd hoped to get autographed. He wasn't keen on Sutherland now, but going to the guy's camp had paved his way to the major league. Whether he won or not, he'd be happy to give Liza some signed cards for the boys going to camp next year.

"And you have to sing," she said.

Crap. Now he *had* to win. There was no way he was going to sing in front of her or anyone else.

"What about you?" She cocked her head and he caught himself checking out the smooth skin along the curve of her neck.

"Hmm," he murmured, as if he hadn't already decided. "If I win, I get to kiss you."

She blushed and quickly looked away. He could've sworn he'd seen a flash of fear in her eyes.

"Out you go, you two," Paige called.

Still wondering about Liza's reaction, Cole stepped into the front of the bakery with her and stopped short when he saw who was there. His heart thudded like a pitch in the dirt. Seated around the two-top tables that had been pushed together to form one big one were Mack and Brenda, Frank, and three sports bloggers Cole recognized. But with them sat John and Sylvia Sutherland.

Shit.

Frank had given him the rundown of who would be coming, and it hadn't included them. *Who invited Sutherland to ruin our pie contest?* Cole couldn't believe such a thought had actually crossed his mind. He never guessed he'd be hoping to win a pie contest, and he sure as hell hadn't thought he'd have to cross paths with Sutherland tonight.

He took a deep breath, reining in his frustration. Sports bloggers were there and watching. Everything he did or said would be fair game, and he and Frank wanted all the press to be about his new relationship.

He glanced at Liza, who smiled at him, innocently beaming. "You invited everyone here?" she asked.

Frank must have invited the Sutherlands. It would make sense, even though Cole didn't like the idea. He remembered Frank saying it was all about the optics. This happy-family gathering with Liza's parents was a good way to convince the bloggers that Cole was serious about her.

"Frank rustled up the judges," he said.

Paige came out of the kitchen with dessert plates, forks, and pink-and-yellow-striped napkins. "I told you the judges would be handpicked and hungry."

Cole and Liza said their hellos to the bloggers, and Cole proudly introduced her to Frank.

"It's nice to meet you, Mr. Price," she said, blushing. The guy was a big-time agent, and she was a true sports fan, so she might've been a little starstruck.

Mack introduced her to Brenda, then they got around to Sylvia. Cole swallowed hard.

"Mom," Liza said. "You remember Cole."

Sylvia opened her arms and gave him a warm hug. For a moment he felt as if nothing had changed, as if years of struggling hadn't shaped him into the person he'd become. "We've missed you," she said with a motherly smile. Her eyes sparkled with sincerity, and he noticed that they were the same shade of green as Liza's.

Cole nodded, working to look pleasant. "Nice to see you again." And he kind of meant that. He'd always been fond of Sylvia. But John was the one he hoped had missed him. Missed every stinkin' stolen base, defensive out, and run he'd scored for the Nationals and not for the Orioles.

John stood next to Sylvia, looking straight at Cole, his lips pressed into a smile. He was several inches shorter than Cole — but that was still pretty tall — and he'd aged a little over the years. Even so, he was still a striking figure, in fighting shape, with a full head of silver hair. Cole faced him, feeling a little sick — like he shouldn't have done so much nibbling and licking the bowl while he'd been baking.

"Dad," Liza said, looking from John to Cole. "I don't think you two need an introduction."

Damn straight...

Cole wanted to throttle Frank for putting him in this position. But Frank hadn't known the history, and Liza and the Sutherlands did come across as the picture-perfect family for Cole to be associated with.

John extended his hand and Cole shook it firmly, wishing he wasn't wearing a chef's apron right then. "Good to see you, Cole," John said, sounding pretty convincing. But Cole had fallen for his fatherly shtick before. "Heck of a season you've got going."

No thanks to you. Cole's pulse pounded in his ears. "It's been a lot of fun."

Liza narrowed her eyes and shifted her gaze from Cole

to her father.

"Ladies and gentlemen," Paige called as she came out of the kitchen balancing a covered pie on a tray in either hand. "It's time for the celebrity pie death match."

Everyone chuckled but Cole, who managed a small smile.

"I'm not a celebrity," Liza said.

"Play along, girl," Paige teased as she set the pies on a cart. "I'm trying to create some drama here." She rolled the cart in front of the table where everyone could see it.

"Some things never change," Liza quipped.

Paige motioned Liza and Cole over to the cart. They stepped behind it, and she stood between them.

"In the left corner," Paige said, "we have Miss Liza Sutherland from Birdland, the home of the Baltimore Orioles. She's made an Os pie that's sure to be a hit with everyone."

Cole groaned at the lame pun, along with several others. "Except me," he joked.

Paige whipped the cover off of Liza's pie. "Liza, tell them about your offering."

Cole got his first look at the competition and was thankful he hadn't had to work with black and orange. But he had to give Liza credit. Her pie was artfully done, even though it looked like something you'd whip up for Halloween. He winked at her, just to let her know he wasn't intimidated.

She smirked at him playfully and straightened her back, looking tough, and he couldn't help thinking about their bet. The girl could smirk all she wanted, but he was still going to get that kiss. He was amazed how real his desire felt in a relationship that was supposed to be fake.

"I started with an Oreo crust," Liza said, "otherwise known as Oriole crust."

Cole shook his head, while everyone chuckled.

"Then I filled it with a mix of vanilla ice cream, vanilla

flavoring, and whipped cream." Liza cupped her hand around her mouth and whispered loud enough for everyone to hear. "I added orange food coloring—"

"That's unnatural!" Cole said.

Liza lifted her hands, palms up. "I mean, come on. Try to make something orange that's not pumpkin or sweet potato."

"Then you would have lost for sure," he teased. He couldn't believe he was having this much fun with Sutherland in the room.

"That's unsportsmanlike," she said with a grin. "Where's a good umpire when you need one?"

Frank hooted, and several others joined in. Paige seemed pleased that everything was going so well. Cole liked seeing Liza so animated and happy. The bloggers were captivated by her, and he could see why.

He was a little captivated himself.

"Then," Liza said, "I added crushed Oreo cookies and brownie bits to the mix, so you have all that yummy texture and a rich vanilla ice cream taste. I topped it with a band of whipped cream with orange sprinkles and put a Sugar Sheet Orioles logo on an Oreo medallion and stood it up in the middle." She gestured toward her pie in a Vanna White kind of way, and everyone clapped and whistled. Cole gave her props, too. Her pie looked good, but he was sure his had hers whipped.

"In the right corner," Paige said after things calmed down, "we have Mr. Cole Collins of Natstown, home of the Washington Nationals. He's knocked it out of the park with his Nats pie."

Everyone groaned again, and Paige giggled.

"Cole, tell them about your pie." She pulled the cover off.

Several people oohed and aahed, and Liza's eyes widened. Cole gave her a gotcha look, and wondered how soon he could get his kiss.

"Wow," Mack said. "That's a heck of a good-lookin' pie. If baseball doesn't work out for you—"

Frank slapped his hand against his heart. "Don't even say that out loud."

"I started with a graham cracker crust," Cole said. "Otherwise known as Nationals crust."

Liza scrunched her nose and shook her head, then she busted out laughing with everyone else. "Those have nothing to do with each other."

Cole nodded. "Now they do."

"Then I mixed up a mean traditional pound cake. You know, butter, eggs, milk, sugar, vanilla—that wholesome all-American stuff—and baked it in the pie crust."

"Then that's not a pie," Liza said. "It's a cake. You're disqualified."

"Yours isn't a pie, either. It's ice cream." Cole grinned. They sounded like five-year-olds. "We've got a double disqualification, or we keep this match alive."

"Fight! Fight! Fight!" one of the bloggers called out—the one Cole would've least expected to join in. The guy had always been kind of quiet and serious behind his rimless glasses and side-parted hair. Everyone but Liza joined in the chant, clapping in rhythm.

She shook her head after the noise died down, an exasperated smile on her face. "Go on. Finish telling us about your cake-pie."

"So then I added a layer of chocolate mousse—"

"You've got to be kidding," Liza said. "It's a mousse-cake-pie?"

"And yours is an ice-cream-cookie-brownie-pie."

Standing between them, Paige shrugged. "I couldn't have scripted this any better." She put her hand on Liza's shoulder.

"Can Cole finish now?"

"Yes." Liza gave him a flirty, knowing look, as if it was inevitable she would lose and he'd be kissing her soon.

Happily distracted by the idea, he scrambled to get himself back in the game. "On top of the mousse is a layer of whipped cream, which made a nice white background for the star in the center—fresh raspberries edged with a double line of fresh blueberries. My round, Sugar Sheet red-on-white curly W logo is stuck on a pick in the middle, marking this as the official mousse-cake-pie of the Washington Nationals."

The group applauded, and Cole nodded appreciatively. "Wait till you taste it." He grinned. "I won't mind if you call me Paula Deen."

Paige raised a shiny silver pie server in front of her. "Judges, those are our contenders. Now it's time to eat some pie and pick a winner."

• • •

Liza tasted both pies, sure that hers would be ten times better than Cole's. But it wasn't. Hers was simple goodness, and she'd have been proud to take it to a potluck. But Cole's was incredible, with its layers of pound cake, chocolate mousse, and whipped cream. Add the graham cracker crust and berries, and his was a grand slam.

Across the room, Cole chatted with Mack and Brenda, looking relaxed and heart-stoppingly hot, all broad-shouldered and blond. Liza might as well be sixteen again. Sometimes she forgot to breathe when she looked at him.

Could she really date Cole for two months and not fall for him? He had everything any girl could want, and he could bake, too. Even so, there was no way she was going to vote for his Nationals pie-cake-mousse-cobbler-whatever. She voted for her Orioles pie. *Go Birds!*

"The votes have been counted," Paige announced, "and I've saved them in case of a lawsuit." She grinned. "Ladies and gentlemen, the smackdown goes to Cole's Nationals pie."

Everyone clapped, and Frank chanted, "Paula Deen, Paula Deen."

Cole grabbed the sides of his apron and did a mock curtsy that had the bloggers clambering for their cameras.

"Was it close?" Liza asked.

Paige grimaced. "Um, ten to one."

"Ten to one?" Liza shot an incredulous look at her mom and dad. "Even my own parents didn't vote for my Orioles pie?" She smiled and shook her head. "What gives? You guys are co-owners of the team."

"Never let it be said that I don't play fair." Her dad slung his arm around her and out of the corner of her eye, she saw a hitch in Cole's expression. But when she looked at him square on, it was gone.

"I'm sorry, sweetie." Her dad patted his stomach. "But that Nationals pie deserved a division title."

"Thanks," Cole said, but didn't look at her dad. He swept his gaze over everyone gathered at the tables. "I was thinking more World Series."

The contest had distracted Liza, but now that it was over, she couldn't think about anything but the kiss she owed Cole.

Her stomach churned. She'd had too much pie, but that wasn't why. The crazy thing was that she *wanted* to kiss him. The battle between guilt and excitement had her torn up inside. Guilt over Wes…guilt over her deal with Frank. And how could she not fall for Cole if he was going to be kissing her and making his All-Star moves? She should've thought a lot further ahead than she had, but she'd been focused on everything BADD could do with Frank's donation. She pinched her eyes closed for a moment. This was her fault. She'd agreed to Frank's terms, and she'd challenged Cole to the bet to begin with.

Liza stepped next to Cole, figuring a coy way to pay up. She stood on her tiptoes and gave him a kiss on the cheek. He smelled like cake, with a tinge of that blue-scented cologne. "Congratulations," she said, loudly enough for others to hear, then whispered in his ear, "You won the bet—that was your kiss."

He casually skimmed his fingers across her lower back and clutched her waist, pulling her close. "There's no chance you're gonna get away with that." His voice was as rich as warm honey and nearly twice as sweet. He gave her a slow-and-easy smile with that perfect mouth, and a flurry of tingles swirled through her. "The bet was that *I* get to kiss *you*."

Liza's heart did a backflip.

They said good-bye to everyone and insisted on helping Paige clean up. She and Liza headed to the kitchen while Cole stayed out front and put the tables and chairs back in place.

"You could've hooked me up with a better recipe," she teased Paige as she wiped the tops of the stainless steel tables in the kitchen. She and Cole had made a mess of the place.

"Yours was scrumptious." Paige ran steaming water into one of the deep sinks, and frothy bubbles rose between the dirty bowls and pans, stacked several high. "And using orange and black was a challenge."

"Remind me to pick my next favorite team based on their colors." Liza joined Paige at the sink and started rinsing the freshly scrubbed pans Paige handed her.

"My heart was on your side." Paige raised her eyebrows suggestively. "But other parts of me were rooting for Cole."

"I know what you mean."

Paige nudged Liza's shoulder. "I say go for it."

"This is only our second date." *And it isn't what it looks like. It's all part of a slimy scheme to help me meet my fund-raising goals.* Liza was thankful Paige wasn't watching her closely. She had an uncanny ability to read Liza's mind.

"So what? You've known the guy since you were sixteen, and crushed on him for years."

Liza shook her head. "You're hopeless."

"Come on. Your friends and family approve—that's pretty obvious. You can't tell me it hasn't crossed your mind."

"I just don't want to make a mistake." She tipped her head toward the front of the bakery where Cole was finishing moving the tables and chairs. "He's dated so many women—I mean, Victoria's-Secret-model kind of women. Now he wants *me*?"

Paige lifted her hand out of the water and flipped it dismissively. Soapsuds splattered against the backsplash. "You've got way more going on than any airhead angel model. Cole's smart enough to see that. And he's with you, isn't he? Jeez—he freakin' *proposed* to you."

"That wasn't real."

"Even so, that stunt with the reporters last night told me he's pretty interested in keeping you around. But then you two came in here today and I saw it for myself. He's crazy about you. And you're crazy if you don't see it."

"Don't see what?" Cole asked from behind them.

Liza's stomach leaped into her throat. She turned so quickly that she almost wrenched her neck. Paige was just a beat behind her.

Cole leaned against the doorjamb, casually folding the apron he'd taken off.

Liza looked at Paige, wide-eyed. *Don't tell him…*

Paige cocked her head Liza's way. "That she's got way more going on than any airhead angel model you might have dated." Paige smirked. "And that you're crazy about her."

Liza wanted to die. But first she wanted to kill Paige. She quickly popped her on the butt with the damp dish towel.

"Ouch!"

"What kind of friend are you?" Liza tried not to laugh out of sheer embarrassment, and she definitely didn't look at Cole.

"The kind who knows her stuff." He walked over to the sink with a lopsided smile on his face.

Liza knew he'd charmed the pants off of who-knows-how-many women, yet she couldn't help but think he really might like her. Maybe Frank had been telling the truth. Though that would make things way more complicated than she had hoped...

Cole ran his tongue across his bottom lip, mesmerizing Liza. "I wouldn't wear an apron for just any girl."

"You should," Paige said. "That hot chef look was really working for you."

"Really?" Cole asked.

"For sure."

He cocked his head and raised his eyebrows at Liza. "You think?"

She shrugged, even though he really was drool-worthy. "If you're into that kind of thing."

He gave her a wounded look.

"She's just pouting because she lost the pie war," Paige said.

"That reminds me." Cole gave Liza a lazy, sexy smile. "We need to finish up and get out of here. We've got a bet to settle."

Chapter Eight

Cole pulled his truck into the dimly lit parking lot across from Nats stadium where Liza had left her car after that day's game. There were only a few vehicles in the dirt lot surrounded by a chain-link fence. He was always struck by how much energy filled the area around game time, and how lifeless it would be just hours later.

"I bet that blue Acura is yours," he said to Liza. She'd been much quieter since they left the bakery and it was just the two of them. After all the fun they'd had today, he didn't get why she seemed so tense now that they were alone. Heck, he didn't get a lot of things about her, but he was glad Frank had picked her.

Maybe once they got that tense first kiss out of the way, she'd calm down—and the Liza he'd known years ago would show up again. He'd gotten glimpses of that girl, so he knew she was still there. She'd teased him with a kiss on the cheek, but she wasn't getting away tonight without making good on their bet.

"How do you know the Acura's mine?" she asked as he pulled in next to it and shifted into park.

"Let's see. There's a pickup and a minivan, two sedans, and a beater. And then there's that shiny little Acura." He nodded and grinned confidently. "It's yours."

She raised her eyebrows. "Fooled you. It's the beater." She jumped out of the truck before he had time to open the door for her, just as she'd done at the end of their date last night.

He got out and hurried around before she had time to get in the Acura and dash off again. She already had her keys in hand. "Then let me walk you to your car." He gestured across the lot to the worn-out Chevy.

She bunched her lips, looking sexy and playful, and he almost kissed her right there. All of a sudden he was even more determined to do it. "Busted," she said. "The Acura's mine." She dangled her keys in front of him. He grabbed them as he would an off-line throw to first base.

"Not so fast. I've got something to show you."

She blinked several times. "That's the best line a player like you can come up with?" she teased, but he could tell she was working hard at it.

He dropped her keys into his pocket. "The only player I am tonight is a baseball player." He'd heard a lot of her conversation in the kitchen with Paige, confirming again that she saw him that way. Everyone did, and he certainly acted like one. He wouldn't need Frank's plan if he didn't.

But for some reason, he wanted Liza to see him differently. Maybe it was because she'd liked him when he was a nobody-teenager or because her parents had felt like family back then. Seeing John and Sylvia tonight had brought all that rushing back to him and made him a little confused.

Liza scanned the bleak parking lot and the nondescript buildings close by, then narrowed her eyes. In the background, a long arch of blue lights stretched along the bridge across the Anacostia River. Wisps of her hair fluttered in the breeze off the water. "So what do you want to show me?"

Cole took her hand, enticed by the delicateness of her slender fingers. He led her out of the parking lot, along the sidewalk on N Street, and to the center-field gate at Nationals Park. There was no one else around, and it was eerily quiet this time of night.

They stopped in the hazy light right in front of the center gate. "I wanted to show you this."

The empty park was alight beyond the promenade and the blue wrought-iron gates with rows of curly Ws down their centers. The beautiful ballpark sat empty and quiet beneath the starry sky. It was a spectacular sight, but intimate, too, since he and Liza stood there alone where thousands of people regularly gathered. Cole loved this view of the park. He'd been with the Nationals since the franchise came to DC, and this place was like home to him.

He glanced at Liza, squeezed her hand, and smiled. She fit in the picture perfectly, looking incredible in the half light with her Nats colors on. "Wow," she said. "This is…"

Cole understood that the words were hard to find—especially if you were a baseball fan. Something about the setting made you all reverent about it.

"I love it," she said with a little awe.

He was happier than he thought he would be that she felt that way about "his" place. He'd figured she would get it, when so many other girls wouldn't. "You make the scene just perfect." He thought he saw her blush, but it was hard to tell in the hazy light.

She gave him a shy smile and quietly said, "Thanks…for showing me this."

"Wanna come back tomorrow? We have an afternoon game, then we leave on a weeklong road trip."

"Really?" She sounded disappointed, and relief coursed

through him.

"We've got three with the Fish, Thursday off, and a weekend with the Phillies." He might be a little disappointed, too. He didn't want to wait that long to see her again.

She stared into the ballpark and kept him waiting for her answer.

Please say yes.

Frank wouldn't like it if she said no again. But Cole would hate it even more.

· · ·

Liza gazed at the view of Nats Park, thinking how awesome it was, and how different it felt than Camden Yards, where the Orioles played. They had a game tomorrow afternoon, too, and she'd have to choose which one to go to.

No shenanigans, Frank had said. She guessed that included saying no when Cole asked her on a date—even though a game wasn't a date.

But she didn't *want* to say no. After tomorrow he'd be gone for a week, and she kind of liked having him around. Today had been fun and easy, and now he'd brought her here tonight to share this rare and incredible view of Nats Park. She could tell he was proud of it—like it was part of who he was. Maybe, after all this time, he'd found a place he belonged.

He squeezed her hand, reminding her he was waiting for her answer. His hand was warm and strong and a little calloused, and it felt comfortable in hers, as if she'd been holding it for years, yet it still felt new and exciting. She figured he was going to kiss her soon—this was a perfect setting for it—and her heart raced at the thought of his lips on hers. How many times had she imagined kissing Cole?

Sorry, Wes. She begged herself not to think about him,

then felt guilty for willing him out of her mind.

"I'll come to your game," she said tentatively, facing him and grasping his other hand.

His mouth quirked up at one corner. "I hear a 'but.'"

"It's an 'and.'" She looked at him coyly. "You have to hit a triple for me."

He drew his head back, his eyebrows lowered. "Not a home run? A triple is kind of a strange thing to ask for. No guaranteed payoff there."

"Hit a triple," she said, "then steal home."

The stunned look on his face made her smile. His jaw clenched as he thought about it. "That's the hardest play in baseball."

And even though I can't wait, kissing you will be one of the hardest things I've done. Liza had unrealistically imagined she'd never kiss another man after she'd lost Wes, and here she was looking forward to it. She'd dreamed about Cole being her first kiss when she was a girl, and in a way, now it was going to come true.

"You're an All-Star." She skimmed her finger down the top buttons of his shirt and poked him lightly between his pecs. "You can do it."

He clutched her hand and pressed it to his chest. She could feel the rhythm of his heart pounding nearly as fast as hers. "I'm a victorious pie warrior, too." The lights sparkled in his eyes and caught his perfect profile in silhouette.

Liza swallowed hard. He was talking about winning the pie war, so the kiss was coming soon. "Everyone liked my pie," she said. "They just liked yours *a little* more."

He gave her a lopsided grin. "C'mon now. It was a total smackdown." He threaded his fingers through her hair and cradled the nape of her neck, sending butterflies flitting down her spine.

Oh, God…

"But this might make you feel better about it." He pulled her toward him gently and kissed her—tenderly…tentatively.

Adrenaline and awareness shot through her. She'd forgotten the sensation of smooth lips on hers, the masculine brush of stubble at their edges. He cupped her face in his hands and took the kiss from tentative to tantalizing, his velvety tongue coaxing her to respond.

Lost in the moment, Liza couldn't stop herself. She'd been so lonely, it had been so long, and she was kissing *Cole*. Just like her hand in his, it felt so familiar and comfortable, yet fresh and exhilarating, simmering with passion and promise. Tingling heat swirled through her. She instinctively wrapped her arms around him, clutching the taut muscles of his back and pulling him closer. He felt so sturdy and strong, so sexy and alive. How had she thought she could live the rest of her life without this?

A siren blared in the near distance, and Cole pulled back. But he stayed forehead-to-forehead with her, his eyes a kaleidoscope of emotions. Desire, surprise…fear? Liza wasn't sure, but she imagined hers looked the same.

"Wow," he said breathlessly.

She gazed into his eyes, feeling as if she were falling. Then reality gripped her by the heart and she stepped back.

"You okay?" Cole gently squeezed her shoulder.

What had she just done? She'd kissed Cole because of an auction date, Frank's deal, and a *bet*. Not because she was in love or even hoping to be. Her breath hitched as she inhaled, the weight of guilt smothering her. Her eyes welled and she blinked quickly, willing herself not to cry. "I need to go home now." A tear slid down her cheek, and she quickly swiped it away.

It was all so fake and confusing. Because that kiss had felt so *real*.

Chapter Nine

Liza went into her parents' house through the back door, just as she did almost every Sunday morning the Orioles were in town and during the off-season. The smoky sweet smell of bacon and French toast filled the air. She inhaled deeply, thinking that no scented candle could ever match the real thing, and that Dorothy had been right in *The Wizard of Oz*... there's no place like home. The feeling of a sure thing was comforting after she'd been so confused and emotional last night.

"French toast today?" she asked, rounding the corner into the large country kitchen. Her mom stood at the stove, and her dad sat at the round kitchen table with newspapers spread all over it, a cup of coffee in his hand.

She kissed her dad on the cheek, feeling like a little girl again when she did.

"Mornin', Slugger." He'd given her the nickname years ago when they'd signed her up for softball and found she couldn't hit.

She crossed the kitchen and hugged her mom.

"We didn't know whether to expect you this morning or

not." Sylvia winked, a glimmer in her eyes. "You and Cole looked pretty cozy last night."

"Mom!" Liza shook her head quickly, blushing. "It's not like that. Besides, I remember a time when you discouraged *that kind* of behavior."

Liza couldn't help but think about kissing Cole last night—she hadn't thought about much else since—and what a wreck she'd been afterward. He'd walked her back to her car and hadn't even made a game of giving her back her keys.

"I don't understand," he'd said as she swept more tears from her face.

She'd shrugged. "I'm not sure I do, either."

Before she'd even gotten back to Baltimore, he tweeted.

Cole Collins @ColeCollins
@LizaSutherland Best bet I ever won. #piewar See you tomorrow…

She had no idea what she was going to do about the mess she'd gotten herself into. But after today, he'd be gone for a week. She could use that time to try to figure it out.

"You two made the *Post* and the *Sun* today." Her dad held up two sections of newspaper.

Liza joined him at the table and had a look. The *Washington Post* had a picture of her kissing Cole on the cheek. The mostly eaten Nationals pie still looked like a pastry chef's creation sitting on the cart in the foreground. The headline read, "Collins Hits Home Run with Nationals Pie."

Liza thought about that literally and smiled, kind of liking the idea of Cole's pie being smacked to smithereens with a baseball bat.

The *Baltimore Sun* had a picture of Cole taking a bite of

Orioles pie, with Liza playfully looking on. They'd gone with the headline, "Orioles Pie Tasty, but Not a Hit with Nationals' Collins."

Both articles detailed some of the funnier moments of the pie war, and gave Sweet Bee's a shout-out, along with information on how people could order the pies.

"Paige will be thrilled," Liza said, happy that she'd gotten some good publicity.

Her mom brought three plates to the table piled with sizzling bacon and golden-brown French toast. "It was a nice thing for Cole to do for her."

Cole's nice… Cole's crazy about you… Cole rocked your world with that kiss. Liza was inundated with reasons to take a chance with him. But memories of Wes filled her heart, and she couldn't shake her guilt over the deal she'd made with Frank. Cole had probably trusted her to be genuine, and look what she'd done to him.

Her mom brought over the warm maple syrup and joined them at the table. Liza quickly took a bite of crispy bacon. The smoky, spicy flavor always reminded her of home. "This is delicious."

"We certainly enjoyed the pie war last night." Her mom looked pleased that she'd used some hip lingo.

"Even though you didn't vote for the Orioles one?" Liza joked.

"Fortunately," her dad said, smiling and gesturing toward the newspapers, "they left that little detail out of those articles."

"It was nice to meet Mack and Brenda," her mom said. "Frank has always been all business with us, so I had no idea how lively he could be. And Mack is so quiet. It's hard to believe they're brothers."

Liza stopped chewing a buttery-sweet morsel of French

toast. "They're brothers?" she asked, covering her mouth.

Sylvia nodded. "That's what Brenda said."

Cole hadn't mentioned that to Liza, although she couldn't think of a reason he would have. She supposed it didn't really make a difference that the two men were related, although she couldn't help but wonder if Mack knew about her deal with Frank. Mack seemed like a salt-of-the-earth kind of guy who would never go for that kind of thing, and he wouldn't think much of Liza for going along with it, either. *And Mack just might tell Cole.*

Liza swallowed hard. Guilt came at her from everywhere. She was leading Cole on, lying to Paige and her parents, and not being true to herself. Her intentions had been good—hadn't they? Frank's donation to BADD would help a lot of kids.

"You missed a tight one yesterday, Slugger," her dad said, referring to the Orioles game. "But we'll take a win any way we can get it, even on an error." He drank some coffee, looking lost in thought and shaking his head. "The Blue Jays are tougher than they were early in the season, though. Wait till you see their lineup today."

Liza hated to tell him and her mom she wasn't going to the Orioles game. She was sure they'd understand, but the games were part of their family routine and they looked forward to going together.

Liza glanced at her mom, who gave her a knowing look, seeming to suspect what Liza was about to say. "Um, Cole asked me to go to the Nats game this afternoon."

Her dad lowered his eyebrows a bit. "Is that what you'd rather do?"

Crap. Had she hurt his feelings? She debated telling them the truth right now and ending all this stress. But then she wouldn't get the donation *or* see Cole again after Frank told him about their deal. "I think so."

A bright smile lit her dad's face. "You really like him, don't you?"

Her parents gazed at her eagerly, thinking she'd reached some meaningful crossroad. She hoped her conflicted emotions didn't show on her face. She might be approaching that crossroad—but right now she was completely lost.

"I like him a little," she said, relieved to tell the truth for a change.

"We do, too." Her mom reached over and squeezed Liza's hand. "We always have, even though we've drifted apart." She gave Liza's dad a sidelong glance.

"Because he got drafted by the Nationals?" Liza asked. "I missed the details on that." She shrugged. "I was too busy with my own drama right about then—with college, and other crushes that didn't turn out so well." She scrunched her face. "But I remember you guys heading down to Chapel Hill a lot during baseball season."

"We bought into the Orioles right before he graduated, and he was busy with the Nationals after he got drafted. It's a shame we lost touch." Her dad frowned ruefully. "Maybe we can make up for some of that lost time with you two hitting it off like you are." They ate in silence for a few moments.

Liza took a deep breath. "The Nats go on a road trip tomorrow, so I'll be back at Camden Yards after work."

"We'll always be there," her dad said. "And we'd always love to have you. Before the end of the season, maybe we can get Cole out to an Orioles game."

"If both teams make the World Series, he'll come to at least a couple of games." Liza said what they were all probably thinking. "But he'll be playing, and we'll have to root against him."

No one said anything as Liza took a swallow of orange

juice. She shrugged, then grinned wickedly. "But it's our turn this time, right? He already won the pie war."

. . .

Cole's phone chirped as he stood at his locker in the Nats clubhouse, getting ready to head out for batting practice. He pushed his hair back from his forehead, put on his cap, and checked for a tweet. Liza had never responded to the one he'd sent last night, so he hoped it was from her.

Paige Ellerbee @SweetBees
@ColeCollins crushes in #piewar. Sorry @LizaSutherland. Rematch?

She'd attached a photo of the article and picture in the paper today. Cole had been glad she'd gotten some good publicity for her bakery, but he hadn't been as happy to see a picture of himself wearing an apron on the *Washington Post*'s home page. His teammates had ragged on him about his and Liza's picture on their hayride and his practice proposal stunt, but they had absolutely *tortured* him about the apron and the pie war — even though he'd won.

He looked up from his phone to see Frank across the room, quickly shaking hands with the shortstop. He turned and headed Cole's way.

Frank gave Cole a hearty pat on the back and a smile that showed most of his teeth. "It's working, son," he said beneath the din of noise in the locker room. He glanced around to see if anyone was within earshot. "Two days in the *Post*, one in the *Sun*. Hayrides and pies. Liza sitting in the stands. Meeting the parents." He gestured toward the heart-shaped collage of Cole and Liza's pictures on the locker room wall. The same smart-ass teammate had blown up a copy of the picture of

Cole in an apron and written "Whipped" in big black letters across the bottom. "Word's getting around that you're serious about her. They're going to be waving that contract like an SOS flag."

"I already knew her parents," Cole said defensively. He was eyeball-deep in this charade that Frank was deftly managing, but he wasn't managing it so well himself. Seeing John and Sylvia yesterday had stirred him up enough. Then there was that kiss with Liza last night.

That mind-blowing, heart-pounding, game-changing kiss.

He couldn't get it out of his head, and he couldn't afford the distraction. Today's game was a must-win, and he needed to be focused on baseball. Why had she cried and practically run away afterward? All Liza, all the time was starting to get to him. Or maybe *she* was starting to get to him.

It was definitely time for a road trip.

Chapter Ten

Cole had managed to focus on the game enough to hit three of four and score the winning run for the Nats in a 2-1 squeaker. The team hit the road tomorrow, so Cole had tonight to figure out what was going on with Liza. Frank's plan might be starting to work the way he'd said, but Cole was more concerned about Liza and what had happened between them. He hated to risk scaring her off, but he was going to do it anyway.

"Where are we headed?" Liza asked, riding shotgun in Cole's pickup as he drove toward the outskirts of DC. He glanced over at her, taking more time than was safe to check her out. She looked pretty hot in a pair of jeans and a fine-knit butter-yellow sweater that had grabbed his attention right away. It begged for him to touch it—all clingy, but tasteful, with a deep V-neck plunging past a lace-trimmed camisole. Windblown from the game, her hair fell in a cinnamon-colored frame around her face and her lips shimmered with a hint of gloss, just waiting to be kissed.

Cole reluctantly turned his attention back to the road. "I'm taking you home."

He'd arranged for Mack and Brenda to pick her up and bring her to the game, so she'd have no way to run off if she got emotional on him again. He would have her all to himself tonight. The idea excited him more than he wanted to admit—as long as there'd be no crying. He remembered the helpless feeling he'd gotten when his grandma cried, worrying about his mother and wishing she'd straighten up.

"You're taking me home?" she asked, looking surprised.

"I thought we'd pick up some dinner and go to your place." He glanced at her quickly, but long enough to see her biting her lip. He reached over, squeezed her hand, and kept hold of it. "I'd love to take you out somewhere, and we can do that, if you want. But sometimes I like a little privacy so I can relax."

Frank wouldn't appreciate that Cole's plan didn't include a public appearance with Liza, but that was just tough crap for Frank. Cole thought she might enjoy doing something quiet. He hoped she'd be comfortable enough at her own place to clue him in on what went wrong last night, just when things had felt so right.

"How about ribs?" she asked.

"Ribs?"

"Yep. Barbecue ribs." She nodded. "There's this little place up the road that looks like a dilapidated log cabin. It's not much better on the inside, but they smoke some mean ribs, and whip up some crazy-good secret-recipe sauce."

Cole raised his eyebrows. He'd been known to drive long distances for a killer rack of ribs.

"What?" Her eyes widened. "Don't tell me you're a vegetarian. I saw you eat a hot dog."

He shrugged.

"Uh-uh." She shook her head. "Those weren't some kind of tofu dogs, were they? No wonder they exploded into flames."

He smiled, wondering where she got her wild ideas. "Sorry, miss. Those dogs were all beef, and the simple fact is you just scorched one."

She pouted playfully, then grinned. "Ribs it is, then. I promise they'll be good, since I'm not cooking."

. . .

Liza's stomach swirled with nervousness as the elevator rose to her floor. The smell of spicy barbecue and fresh hush puppies filled the air quickly. Cole leaned casually against the wall, carrying two giant white paper bags that held their dinner. She couldn't help but notice how his loose jeans hung perfectly over his long legs and narrow waist. And the man could rock a polo shirt. Cole's was Carolina blue, and just snug enough to hint at the cut of muscles underneath. The color made his eyes look lighter. His hair swept across his collar like a field of summer wheat against a clear blue sky. Liza could hardly believe how lucky she was that he was here with her, especially after she'd run away last night. He had to wonder why she'd done that…again.

She had mixed feelings about him coming to her place, but she understood his reasoning. The privacy issue wasn't arguable. She'd seen the way fans acted when they came across a big-name athlete in public. Besides, a normal dating couple would want to spend time alone—right? But they weren't a normal dating couple…even though Cole didn't know that. He was probably just being considerate of her and trying to move things forward.

Liza's insides were in a knot by the time she opened the door to her condo and Cole followed her inside. He stopped a few steps in, and she took the bags from him while he quickly checked out the place. She'd decorated it in taupe and serene blue, with an ivory accent here and there. Not ultramodern like the decorator had suggested, but cozy contemporary and comfortable. She hadn't wanted it to be a showplace; she just wanted it to feel like home.

His gaze settled on the harbor view. "Home *sweet* home." He seemed to like the setting and the view. He stepped over to the wall of windows that flanked the balcony doors and practically pressed his nose against one of them.

Liza set the bags on the granite countertop of the island that separated the kitchen from the living area. "We can eat on the balcony if you want."

He nodded like an excited little kid, even though he was an incredibly rich pro baseball player who could afford places almost anywhere with much more stunning views than hers. For a quick moment, she imagined what he must have looked like as a little blue-eyed, blond-headed boy, excited about his first baseball game.

"And here I thought I might have been showing you something by taking you out to the storybook farm," he said.

"Are you kidding?" She got the food ready to serve. "I'd trade this view for the farm any day."

She grabbed a couple of cold beers from the fridge, and he helped her take their dinner out on the balcony. They lit several candles, sat down next to each other, facing the view, and spread their feast out on the table—mac 'n' cheese, green beans with ham, golden-brown hush puppies, and ribs glazed with sauce. She couldn't wait to dig in.

He grabbed several napkins from a big pile. "This is going to be messy."

"That's half the fun." She reached for a hush puppy and took a crispy bite.

He did the same, and they split the racks of ribs. Liza

absently licked the sauce from her fingers, one-by-one.

"I could help you with that," he said with a sexy glint in his eyes and a seductive curve of his lips.

Mmm...he's irresistible. She swallowed hard.

"I'm good," she said lightly, and fluttered her fingers at him. But then she imagined him sensuously licking her fingers, and she considered dunking them back in the sauce.

Cole raised one eyebrow, as if he had heard her thoughts, then tore into one of the ribs and chewed with a look of pure bliss on his face.

"Holy Hannah, these are good." He took another hearty bite.

Liza chuckled. "Did you just say holy Hannah? Paige says that sometimes, but I can't believe that's how you talk in the dugout."

He shook his head, still chewing. After he swallowed, he said quietly, "My mom used to say it because my grandma didn't allow cussing in her house."

The breeze off the harbor caught the corners of their napkins. "What happened to your mom?" she asked sympathetically.

Even in the candlelight Liza could see the sadness in his eyes. He took a long time to answer. "Every one of her Mr. Rights were Mr. Wrongs. Before her drinking got too bad, she dated a decent guy or two, but they weren't interested in anything serious with a girl who had a little kid and worked part-time stocking groceries at Piggly Wiggly. So she took up with rough guys who drank with her, then beat her."

Liza's heart hitched, thinking about how difficult that had to have been for him and his grandma.

He swiped his napkin across his mouth and gazed into the distance. Moonlight glinted on the water, and the occasional blinking lights of airplanes twinkled like moving stars. "When I was thirteen, I went after her boyfriend, but she managed to get between us before too much damage was done. She didn't come around too much after that."

This was the Cole she remembered, who'd easily talked to her about almost anything, even though it was difficult. But now she could see how life had turned out for him, and why he seemed a little lonely under all that swagger. She smoothed her fingers up and down his forearm. "That had to be tough."

He shrugged, stretching the fabric of his shirt tightly across his broad shoulders. "As long as those guys took her to Atlantic City once in a while, she'd stay with them. She'd call sometimes to tell me and my grandma she was headed to the casinos, and she was finally going to hit it big."

Liza took his hand and laced her fingers between his. He looked so perfect in the candlelight with his strong jaw, high cheekbones, and that trademark mole—with a hint of vulnerability in his eyes. No one ever would have guessed he hadn't had a perfect life to match. She brought his hand to her lips and kissed it tenderly. "Your mom had already hit it big when she had you."

He gave her a wan smile and shifted his gaze toward the water. "I don't think she saw it that way," he said quietly. "One rainy night she and her drunk boyfriend left a bar on his motorcycle. The guy took a curve too fast and slid out of control. He made it, but my mom didn't."

Liza's heart ached for him. He'd told her a bit about his background when they'd been teenagers, but she hadn't imagined the story had turned out like this.

She clutched his tightly muscled shoulder, trailed her hand down his arm, and hooked her fingers in the crook of his elbow, aware of the heat of his skin beneath her touch. "I'm sorry that happened to her…and you…and your grandma."

"My grandma was really more like a mom to me." He twisted his napkin between his long fingers. "She packed sandwiches in my lunch that she'd cut with a biscuit cutter, and told me they were baseball PB and Js. She said if I ate them, I'd play better." He shook his head and a lock of silky hair fell across his forehead. "I believed her. And I had round sandwiches in my lunch until I went to high school."

Liza smiled. "I wish I could have met your grandma. She sounds like my kind of lady."

"I think you two might be a lot alike." He grinned, and popped a hush puppy into his mouth. "Only she could really cook."

. . .

"I know how to make reservations," Liza joked.

Cole rolled his eyes, relieved they were back to casual conversation. Liza was so easy to talk to that he might just spill his whole life story—secrets and all—if he wasn't careful.

"And I know how to make Orioles pie." She nodded as if that were some huge accomplishment. From what he had seen, it probably was. "Paige says she has orders all the way through the World Series."

"For Nats pies or Orioles?"

"Both."

"That'll be sad," he said, and picked up another rib.

"What?"

"Orioles fans eating their fake-orange pie, watching the Nats play another team in the Series." He raised one shoulder. "But ice cream is good comfort food, so there's that."

"Just wait." She lifted her chin. "Both of our teams might be in the Series."

Or neither of them.

Cole chased the thought out of his head. He of all people knew how negative thinking could sabotage things. "That'd be good. Especially if it goes down like our pie war did."

"Not a humble winner, are you?"

He skimmed his fingertips across the top of her hand. "Not when the stakes are that high." *Like they are with the Nats and me.* As the end of the season drew closer, he was getting more and more worried about landing another contract. Yet the more time he spent with Liza, the guiltier he felt about using her to get it. He hated to think how hurt she would be if she found out about Frank's plan. Cole had seen her in tears last night, and he didn't want to upset her like that again. "Why were you crying last night?"

Her expression tightened for a second, then a corner of her mouth turned up. "Doesn't that always happen when you kiss girls?"

He wouldn't let her joke this away. He couldn't afford for things to go wrong now…and he didn't want them to. He was leaving for a week, and he had to know where he stood.

"I have to admit that was a first," he said seriously. He dragged his hand down his face and searched for the right words. The last thing he wanted was to strike out here. "I don't understand."

She stared at her plate for what seemed like minutes. Candlelight glowed on her face and flickered in her eyes. She looked simply gorgeous.

"Two years ago…" Her voice wavered. "I was engaged."

Cole blinked rapidly as a rogue streak of envy tore through him. What kind of guy had she been engaged to? *And what kind of guy would leave her?*

"His name was Wes Kelley," she said, as if she'd read his mind. "He was a Secret Service agent." She nervously twisted the chain of her delicate silver bracelet between her fingertips. "We were friends. Then we fell in love and he proposed. We'd planned a spring wedding."

Cole expected her to keep talking, but she didn't. She just kept twisting her bracelet.

"But you never got married," he said.

"No," she whispered. "He was killed on the job. He jumped in front of a bullet that was meant for a visiting third-world dictator."

Cole put his arm around her and pulled her close. "I am so sorry." She rested her head on his shoulder and he caught the fresh, flowery scent of her hair. "I had no idea."

They sat quietly for a little while, giving him time to enjoy the feel of her in his arms and to wrap his head around her story. Things were starting to make more sense. No wonder she'd been so guarded with him at times. The fun Liza he'd seen was the real Liza, coming back from all kinds of hell.

Cole wondered if Frank had known about that part of her past. He couldn't imagine the guy would intentionally put her in a position to get her heart crushed again. The scary thing was that Cole couldn't imagine himself doing that, either.

Man, what a mess.

Liza pulled away, took a deep breath, and said, "I know it's been two years, but I just wasn't ready to date." She shrugged weakly. "My mom is so certain there's someone else out there…"

"And she thought it might be me?" he asked. It was obvious that Sylvia wanted him and Liza to get together, since she'd bid on the BADD date. But he hadn't understood why—especially considering how she and John had disappeared from his life.

"I'm not sure. She knew I liked you years ago. But people change."

Had he changed that much? Sure, he'd become a pro baseball player who looked to all the world as if he didn't want for anything. But he was still so alone—especially since his grandma died, and Sylvia and John left him. All he really wanted was a simple life with someone who loved him, and all he'd done by acting like a playboy was make sure he didn't get it.

She swept her hand across her forehead, then tucked her hair behind her ear with a swipe of her delicate fingers. "I'm just really confused."

"About what?" He hated asking because he already knew the answer. And he knew he was the reason she felt that way.

"We went on a charity auction date," she said. "I understood that from the start, and I played along. But it had to be awkward for you, wondering which Liza was going to show up from minute to minute." She shook her head. "I'm just all over the place."

"It makes sense to me now," he said. "I wish you would've told me." But if she had, he never would have gotten in this deep with her. He'd have kept going on with his lonesome life and missed that spark of hope that was trying to catch fire in his heart. Hope for a new contract...*and* hope for something more.

"Then you asked me out again and—"

"You shot me down," he said lightly.

She gave him a small smile. "I saw the error of my ways." She glanced at him self-consciously. "But that kiss," she said. "I haven't kissed anyone since Wes. Hadn't even thought about it."

"I didn't know," he said.

Liza shook her head, and a lock of her hair fell over her shoulder and along the deep vee of her sweater. She absently traced her fingers along it, over the swell of her breast, and twisted the end between her fingertips. Cole inhaled sharply. The girl had no idea how sexy she was.

"I just didn't imagine it would be like...that." She set her green-eyed gaze on him, and he knew exactly what she meant. "That's why I'm confused."

He nodded. "I promise that makes two of us."

They ate almost all the food, then cleared the table and went inside. The air had gotten prickly-cool, and the breeze had become billowy, bringing in clouds. Cole kept the conversation light, and she seemed to appreciate that. There'd been enough seriousness for one night.

Liza tuned the TV to baseball highlights while they straightened the kitchen. Analysts previewed the Nats game against the Marlins in Miami, where Cole would be tomorrow.

"We could clinch the division title on this trip." He'd hesitated to say it out loud for fear it might jinx them.

She finished rinsing the dishes, looked him in the eyes, and smiled. "I hope you do."

He could've sworn she meant it.

"What's on your agenda this week?" he asked.

"Just work and a couple Os games." She wiped the countertops, leaving the kitchen as gleaming as it was when they'd arrived.

He leaned against the counter and she faced him, her expression bright. "BADD's expanding the camp program next year, so I've got lots of details to work out—budgets and logistics. All that exciting stuff."

"You seem excited about it."

"I am. I love that part of my job. Especially since I've seen some of the boys who have come through get college scholarships. A couple of really talented guys got drafted. Their stories are just amazing." She didn't have to tell Cole that. His story was one of them.

He tucked his chin and lightly skimmed his fingers from her shoulder to her elbow. "You're amazing." *Boy, Frank would love that line.* But Cole realized he meant it.

And that scared the hell out of him.

She blushed quickly beneath those sexy freckles. "You're not so bad yourself," she said shyly.

Cole knew he shouldn't risk kissing her again, but he had to know if he'd imagined the fireworks between them last night. He gently put his arm around her, splaying his hand across the small of her back. She gazed at him with questions lingering in her pale-green eyes, her lush lips parted. Pulling her to him, he lightly touched his lips to hers. Soft and supple. Satiny and smooth. Just the feathery wisp of his mouth on hers sent desire pulsing through him.

He worried she would pull away, but she didn't. She lifted her chin and took his face in her hands, deepening their kiss with the sensuous sweep of her tongue.

Holy... Last night's kiss began to pale in comparison. Cole twined his fingers in her silky hair, stirring the scent of wildflowers, and cradled her head in his hand.

She clutched the tense muscles along his back. Arching against him, she whimpered, and it might have been the hottest sound he'd ever heard.

The things I could do with this woman...

Could he afford to get involved with her and her grief and her parents? He'd just wanted a new contract. But this kiss could lead places he knew he shouldn't go...

Get a hold of yourself, man.

She had his blood pumping more than a full-count pitch with the bases loaded and the game on the line. He wasn't supposed to *want* her.

He tipped his head back, stared at the ceiling, and tried to get a grip. She pulled away a little, and when he looked at her, she was biting her lip. If he stayed here any longer, he wouldn't be able to resist her. And that would screw up everything.

"We leave early tomorrow," he said. "So I'd better go."

She nodded. "I understand. It's a big week for you."

"Will you be watching my games?" he asked, sounding selfish but hoping she'd say yes.

She raised her eyebrows playfully. "Should I?"

"I'm still working on your triple...and stealing home."

She looked at him demurely. "Then the least I could do is set my DVR."

Chapter Eleven

Liza sat at her desk at the foundation, glancing between the budget spreadsheet on her computer screen and the rain falling outside in the cozy courtyard behind the foundation's town house headquarters. A squirrel scurried up one of three ginkgo trees that shaded beds brimming with orange mums. She couldn't concentrate for thinking about Cole and the time they'd spent together before he left. Her insides tingled when she imagined the softness of his lips on hers, the ripple of his muscles beneath her touch.

A sharp rap on her open office door made her flinch. She turned to see Ross Hinsler, the foundation's CEO, standing there with a file folder in his hand and a strained-looking smile on his face. Ross was a family man in his mid-forties who stayed fit and young-looking, even though gray had started to lighten his dark hair. Business *and* baseball savvy, he ran BADD as if he were managing a major league team. He e-mailed everyone quotes about peak performance and achieving excellence, and seemed to hold himself to the same high standards.

"Hey, Liza," he said. "Got a second?"

It became clear that wasn't a question when he stepped inside, closed the door to a crack, and sat in the chair adjacent to her desk. Her office was so small that if she swiveled her chair just so, it would put them almost knee-to-knee. She brushed a speck of lint off the lapel of her jacket and kept her chair still. He glanced at her computer screen. "Working on numbers?"

Not a question, either. She nodded anyway. He seemed to be trying hard at being casual, and that made her really nervous. She took a swallow of her stone-cold coffee and winced.

Ross opened the file folder he was carrying and cleared his throat. Liza figured what was coming because this scene was a rerun of the one they'd had last year about this time.

"I'm concerned you're not making enough progress toward your fund-raising goals," he said. "The auction was a huge success, so we'll be upgrading the anti-doping programs for players, and the summer camps."

"That's pretty exciting," she said, hoping to steer the conversation toward the camps.

"But everyone still needs to meet their individual fund-raising goals," he said. "Right now, you're much further behind than any of your coworkers."

The inspirational quote he'd e-mailed them this morning said, "Think beyond the boundaries." Right now Liza was thinking beyond the boundary of her office door, and wishing she were on the other side of it. She hated to disappoint Ross. "I'm concerned, too, and I'm working on developing some new donors right now."

"That's good to hear." He shifted in his chair and frowned. "You do a fine job with the camps, Liza. Phenomenal, really. But if you don't make your goals, it's not fair to everyone else who has to raise money, too. It affects all of us—financially and with morale. Especially since the goal sheets are posted in the conference room for everyone to see." He closed the folder and ran his fingers up and down the edge of it. "If you miss your goal two years running, it wouldn't be right for me not to take serious action."

Liza's stomach pitched. "What does that mean?"

"It's a touchy situation with Sylvia being your mom, and you doing so well with the camps. But I'd have to consider some kind of probationary period where you focus on development and someone else runs the camps until you can properly balance your work."

He might as well have slapped her in the face. She couldn't think of a word to say. Running those camps and helping those kids toward their dreams was one of the most meaningful parts of her life.

"Chin up," he said as he stood and opened the door. "You've still got three months, give or take. I know you can do it." He shot her an encouraging smile, and she nodded numbly.

Ross headed down the hall and she spun her chair to face the window. Rain fell steadily outside, weighing down the leaves of the ginkgo trees and making them look sad. She felt the same way. If Ross turned camp management over to someone else, she might never get that job back. Even if she did, everything she'd worked so hard to put into place might be changed or even ruined. Whoever he gave the job to might be just as bad at it as Liza was at fund-raising. Or should she say BADD at it? Though that wasn't even funny right now.

There was always the solution of having her mom intervene, but Liza refused to entertain that option. Regardless of her good intentions, her mom had made things uncomfortable enough for Liza with her coworkers. She was determined to prove herself without the help of her parents.

Liza propped her elbows on the desk. She bowed her head, combed her hands through her hair, and clutched the back of her head where a headache was settling in. She didn't need to worry, really. Everything would be fine. She'd be getting Frank's donation in a couple of months.

Right?

She absolutely couldn't fall for Cole. Yes, she liked him, but she wasn't anywhere near in love with him, and that's what Frank's ridiculous paperwork had said. She and Cole could be friends, couldn't they?

"Trying to keep your head from exploding?"

Liza sat up straight and swiveled her chair. Paige stood leaning against the doorjamb, wearing all black except for a lightweight pink-and-yellow-striped scarf. A large pink tote bag, about half her size, hung from her shoulder.

"Hey," Liza said, trying to act happy. "What are you doing here?"

"I had a delivery a couple miles away, so I thought I'd stop in." Paige lowered her eyebrows. "What's wrong? You look kinda pale."

Liza stood and closed the door. "Ross just told me if I didn't make my fund-raising goal this year, he'd put me on probation and assign someone else to run the camps while I learned to troll for money." The words raced from her mouth, strung together with barely a pause.

"Get out."

"That's just it. I'll *have* to leave here if all he wants me to do is raise money."

Paige narrowed her eyes. "Where is his office? I'm gonna tell him what a dumb—"

Liza's heart leaped into her throat. "No!" She jumped between Paige and the door. Paige was enough of a firebrand to actually go after Ross.

Paige crossed her arms in a huff. "Stop being stubborn and ask your folks for the money. You know they'd donate it."

"I need to prove myself without anyone else's help, just like you're doing with Sweet Bee's. And don't even think about suggesting I get my mom to save my job. I'd have zero credibility around here, assuming I have any now. I just need to raise the money."

"How much are we talking about?"

Liza pinched her eyes closed, and she could hardly look at Paige when she opened them. "Thousands."

"Hmm…that's probably over my budget, but I can help. I'll give you the profits from my pie war sales."

Liza was touched by Paige's generosity. She hugged her, surprised as always at how delicate she felt compared to how she acted. "I couldn't take your money."

"Why not? I've gotten lots of orders."

"That's fantastic," Liza said. This had to be the first time anyone had been interested in anything edible she'd made. "And your offer means a lot to me—you have no idea how much. But I have a prospect that might be good for a big donation." She was dying to tell Paige about her deal with Frank, even though she was embarrassed she'd agreed to do something so underhanded. But she'd sworn to keep it confidential. Paige would never tell on purpose, but sometimes her mouth got ahead of her memory and she blurted out things before catching herself. Liza couldn't risk Cole finding out what she had done.

"Let me know," Paige said. "My offer still stands."

"Aw, thanks." Liza sank back into her chair.

"Maybe this will cheer you up." Paige whipped the cutest cellophane-wrapped cake pop out of her tote, decorated like a mini pumpkin all the way down to the stem.

"That's so precious." Liza took it. "But how am I supposed

to eat it?"

Paige scrunched her face. "It's on a stick. Seems like you could figure it out."

"I know how to eat it. I mean, it's too cute to eat."

Paige quickly pulled out a twin to the first one and handed it to Liza. "Eat this one, then. I need to know how they taste."

"Paige! Didn't you taste them?"

"Sure I did. But I eat this stuff all the time. My taste buds are getting numb to it. They're in permanent sugar-shock."

Liza carefully removed the cellophane from the cake pop, admiring the detailed stem and leaf on the pumpkin. "It's too perfect to mess up."

"I forget I'm dealing with Goldilocks here. It's too cute, it's too perfect. Just eat the stupid thing."

Liza swallowed against the shock of hearing Wes's nickname for her. She'd been so focused on Cole and her job and her deal with Frank that she hadn't been thinking about Wes nearly as much. But right now, the thought of him made her angry. She hated it when that happened, because later she'd feel so guilty. But if Wes hadn't left her, she wouldn't be in this predicament. Now she was all twisted up inside, and her parents and Paige thought she was moving forward with Cole. Well, they were all in for a big surprise, because she was desperate for Frank's donation—more now than ever.

She crumpled the cellophane in her fist and took a bite of the cake pop. The chewy-brownie-textured cake tasted rich, with cream cheese icing perfectly complementing the chocolate. "Delicious," she murmured through a mouthful.

Paige sighed with relief. "Good to know. One bad batch of something, and that could be it for Sweet Bee's."

"I don't think you have anything to worry about."

Paige pushed a stack of files out of the way and sat cross-legged on Liza's desk.

"Make yourself comfortable," Liza teased.

"I owe you and Cole big time." Paige looked serious for once. "For all that publicity Sweet Bee's got from the pie war. Those orders came in so fast I thought about putting an ad on Craigslist for some Oompa Loompas."

Liza was thrilled to see Paige's business doing so well. She'd had a rough go of it since her career as assistant pastry chef at the storied Hay-Adams hotel in DC came to an unexpectedly quick end. Her mom had been diagnosed with lung cancer, and caring for her had been too much for Paige's dad, who ran the barbershop in tiny Maple Creek. So Paige had moved back home to help. She'd still been only an hour from DC, and she could've kept the job. But caring for her mother took most of her time. After her mom passed away, Paige didn't have the heart to leave her dad, so she'd rented the building next to the barbershop and opened Sweet Bee's.

"Have you got more orders than you and Cynthia can handle?" Liza asked, referring to Paige's part-time help.

"I think we'll be okay. The orders are spread out pretty well. But if the Nats or the Os make the World Series, I might need Willy Wonka's whole factory."

"You mean *when* the Nats *and* the Os make the Series." Liza finished eating what was left of the yummy cake pop. The sugar alone was making her feel better about things.

"That'll be awkward," Paige said. "You and Mr. All-Star sexing it up while his team plays your dad's team in the World Series."

"We're not 'sexing it up.'"

"Sorry to hear that," Paige teased. "But you will be soon. For sure by the time the Series rolls around, unless there's simply no freakin' hope for you."

"I can't imagine we'll make it that far."

"What? He all but admitted he's crazy about you. You've

only gotta say the word, and it's *on*." Paige twirled her pink-striped ponytail around her finger. "You have to hit it with Cole-His-Hotness-Collins at least once so you'll have a story to tell your grandkids."

Liza pressed her lips together tightly. "I don't think I could do that to Wes."

"You wouldn't be doing anything to Wes," Paige said softly. "You'd be doing something for you. I'm so incredibly sorry but…hon, Wes isn't here anymore. You've gotten used to grieving him, and sticking with that is painful, but it's easier than taking a risk with Cole."

Liza mulled over what Paige had said, wondering if she were right. Grieving Wes had been the center of her life for two years. It was what she *knew*. But it was sad and lonely, sharing her days with a ghost. The time she'd spent with Cole—when she'd let go and enjoyed herself—had been thrilling and just plain fun. And kissing him… She swallowed hard.

"You need to just do it," Paige said. "Everyone seems to like him, at least everyone who came to the pie war. And all his fans. And me. I *really* like him."

"Easy over there," Liza joked. "He *is* a little likable, even with all that swagger."

"If you were him, you'd have swagger, too. Look what he's accomplished."

Liza couldn't argue. "He's a lot like my dad."

"Women marry men like their dads."

"Whatever. Are you going to marry a barber?"

"Snippy, aren't you?"

Liza rolled her eyes. "Maybe Cole and my dad are too much alike. Did you notice a weird vibe between them at the pie war?"

Paige thought about it as she strung several paper clips into a chain. "Nope. Guess I was too busy to pick up on it, *if anything even happened.*" She gave Liza a stern look. "It sounds like you're digging for something else to keep you from getting closer to Cole."

Liza wondered if that was it. Did she really need anything else? She *did* have her comfort zone grieving Wes, the possible loss of the job she loved, and five hundred thousand other reasons to keep her from falling for him. Why add something else? "I'm not, really."

Paige gave her a sly smile. "Then prove it."

. . .

Cole needed to blow off some steam. After two nights behaving himself in Miami, and two wins for the Nationals, they'd lost to the Marlins when they could've clinched the title—thanks to an error he made. His manager always said every play mattered in the win or loss, and one play couldn't be blamed for the outcome. Cole bought into it when one of his teammates botched a play. But when it was his fault, that theory was bullshit.

How did I miss that damn throw? Lapses in concentration like that reminded him of his struggles in the minor league, and the blown plays that happened in his nightmares.

Cole had decided to stay in his cookie-cutter hotel room and sulk while his buddies went out and grabbed something to eat. He wasn't hungry, and he didn't want to commiserate about a loss he probably could've saved. Had his head been totally in the game?

Propped against several pillows on the bed, he played solitaire on his laptop, trying to distract himself. But he wasn't really paying close attention and he quickly blew the game. *Great—two-for-two tonight.* He tipped his head back and stared at the ceiling, thinking about Liza—because he couldn't concentrate on anything else, especially since she'd told him the story of her fiancé. Unable to ignore his curiosity any longer, he clicked out of solitaire, Googled Wes Kelley, and followed several links.

It didn't take him long to understand what Liza had seen in Wes. The guy had played college baseball at UVA—against Cole's UNC team—then joined the Secret Service after he graduated. From what Cole read in the obituary and other tributes, Wes had been well-liked, smart, and funny. What a waste that he'd died protecting a scummy dictator who'd been on a controversial visit to the US. To make things even worse, the dictator had been assassinated a few months later. Wes had been heralded as a hero, and rightfully so.

Cole clicked on a few more links and came across some engagement photos of Wes and Liza. They'd been taken by one of the rare talented photographers who could capture real emotions with a camera. Cole caught himself envying Wes for the way Liza looked at him in the pictures—with a sparkle of sincere devotion in her eyes. No wonder she was cautious now.

Cole got up, grabbed a Gatorade out of the mini-fridge, and drank half of it in three huge gulps. This night wasn't getting any better. He'd lost the game for the Nats, and now he was knotted up with envy of a fallen hero. Liza would never look at him the way she'd looked at Wes in those pictures—especially if she found out about Frank's plan. He slugged some more Gatorade and his phone rang. He glanced at the caller ID.

Nikki Barlow.

It might as well have said *Trouble.* Frank would rip him a new one if he knew Cole had forgotten to block Nikki's number after their recent run-in with the cops. He hadn't heard from her since, so he wondered why she'd piped up tonight of all nights. Even so, he didn't intend to find out. He let the call go and clicked through Liza's engagement photos again, torn between sorrow for her and Wes, and envy of what he saw between them.

His phone rang again. *Nikki.* Man, things must be slow in Hollywood tonight. He ignored her call only to get a text from her seconds later.

Call me. I need ur help!!

Cole couldn't imagine why she needed his help, but she might be in trouble. No doubt she had plenty of people she could turn to, but for some reason, she'd picked him. He hated to think what might happen if he ignored her. He hesitated as long as his conscience would let him, then called her. Frank wouldn't like it, but he wouldn't have to know. Certainly talking to Nikki on the phone wasn't going to stop the Nats from offering Cole a new contract. Hell, if he kept making errors like he did tonight, they probably wouldn't want him anyway.

"Hi, sexy," Nikki answered, not sounding the least bit troubled. The base beat of a hip-hop tune thrummed in the background. "Saw the game on TV. Bummer."

Not a good start. "For sure," he said, hoping she'd leave it at that. "You need my help with something?"

"Yep. I'm in Miami, too—havin' a little party out on the Venetian Islands. I need you to get on over here."

"You're not in trouble?"

"The only trouble is I'd rather be clubbing in South Beach, but I gotta keep a low profile for a while. This party's just a few drinks. I can't risk gettin' busted again. Sorry 'bout that, by the way."

"Me, too." The drama with Nikki sure hadn't helped his case with the Nats. He wasn't even sure why he'd bothered with her in the first place.

"I definitely owe you one," she said sweetly. "So why don't you come hang out with me?"

"I don't think so, Nik." Most men would question his sanity for turning down Nikki Barlow, but it came out of his mouth with no hesitation.

"Aw, c'mon. You have to be feeling a little down…"

…after how you played in the game tonight.

"You deserve to relax a little," she said.

He did, didn't he? But he shouldn't… "I appreciate the invite, but I'm just gonna hang in my room."

"Please, Cole. I really feel bad about what happened. Let me treat you to a drink or two."

He could use a drink or two. And spending a few hours relaxing with a small group might help him get his head back in the game. Cole hesitated, but then said, "I can probably make it for a little while."

"I'll text you the address," she said. "Hurry."

Cole opened his suitcase and pulled out a decent pair of jeans to wear, knowing he should think this through before he went. But he didn't want to *think* any more tonight.

He took a cab out to the island, second-guessing himself all the way, but not enough to change his mind. It was a private party. Frank would never know. *And neither will Liza.* The cab stopped in front of a huge two-story villa, all lit up outside, with an ornate, cut-glass front door. Cole paid the driver and got out. He stood and gazed at the house as the cab pulled away, the muted thrum of bass reverberating in the balmy sea breeze. He'd expected to be more relaxed by now, and ready to party. But he'd started thinking about how bad things turned out the last time he saw Nikki, and wondering why he'd even want to see her again.

Cole vividly remembered the night they'd had their run-in with the cops. He'd been seduced by the idea of being with *Nikki Barlow*—the woman whom literally millions of men fantasized about every day. But she hadn't been all that, really, with her slurred words and revealing clothes, and her messy dyed-black hair and heavy makeup. She wasn't anywhere near as fresh and sexy as Liza, who was always tastefully dressed, with her silky hair shimmering. Cole loved Liza's look—beautiful with little makeup on and those freckles dotted lightly across her nose. But it wasn't just how she looked that kept him thinking about her. She still knew him better than anyone, and she'd given him a chance in spite of her own struggles. He wondered what would happen if he just let go and allowed himself to fall for her. Was it possible for him to give up the lifestyle he'd been hiding behind and commit to something meaningful?

Most men probably thought he lived a fantasy life with his success in baseball, all his wealth, and plenty of willing women. But those girls only wanted him for money and fame. They'd been easy to find and hard to get rid of sometimes, but that was the only choice he had. He couldn't settle down with one woman. It simply hadn't been an option. In his position, he could never be sure if a girl was sincere. So he'd kept things light and he'd kept things changing and he'd kept everything to himself.

But now there was Liza. Taking a chance with her daunted and excited him, but he was ready to start right now. He stared at the villa and everything became clear. Liza was definitely more important to him than going to any party, no matter how many Hollywood starlets were there.

Cole turned away from the villa, walked a few blocks until he reached the Venetian Causeway, and called a cab. He waited, hoping the cops wouldn't pick him up for loitering, and texted Nikki. *Can't make it tonight after all. Thanks for the invite.* And then he blocked her number from his phone.

After a few minutes of staring into the distance, he took a picture of the view over the water of Miami Beach beneath a starry sky, and attached it to a tweet.

Cole Collins @ColeCollins
@LizaSutherland A girl without freckles is like a night without stars. Wish you were here…

Frank would love that one. But Cole hadn't done it for Frank, or the hope of a new contract with the Nats. He'd sent the tweet for himself—and Liza—and just hoped she was awake to see it.

The cab arrived pretty soon after that. Cole got in and gave the driver his hotel's address. Within minutes, his phone chirped.

Liza?

He glanced at the screen and his stomach clenched.

Nikki Barlow @CrazyNikkiB
Hey @ColeCollins Wish you woulda stayed tonite. Now U owe me 1.

Shit. She must have seen him outside the villa.

· · ·

Cole hadn't even made it to the hotel before Frank called. No doubt he'd seen Nikki's tweet. The guy never missed *anything.* Cole wondered how he had the time and energy to keep up with all the athletes he represented—all the way down to their Twitter accounts. It crossed Cole's mind that most of them probably didn't worry Frank the way he did.

"Hey," he said, gazing out the window as the cab whisked through Miami.

"Wanna tell me about that tweet from Nikki Barlow?" Frank asked in a fed-up tone.

Cole heard a television in the background. He imagined Frank sitting in a big leather chair in the great room of his sprawling Northern Virginia home, watching West Coast ball games on several flat screens mounted on the wall. His place was like a country club sports bar.

"Not really," he said. "I got it under control."

"The hell you do, son." Ice cubes clinked into a glass. *Time for another scotch.* "Does getting another contract with the Nationals really matter to you? Because takin' up with Nikki Barlow is about the quickest way to ensure that you won't."

Cole had known he was making a stupid decision to go anywhere near Nikki's party. At least he'd gotten his head straight and stopped himself before he went in the villa—but not before she had seen him. He raked his hand through his hair. "I'm not taking up with Nikki."

"That's just what the honchos at the Nats need to see— you gettin' tweets from Crazy Nikki saying she wished you'd spent the night." Frank sounded righteously pissed. "And what's Liza gonna think when she sees it? What respectable girl would want to touch you after you'd been foolin' around with that Hollywood trash?"

"We weren't fooling around," Cole said. "I didn't even see her."

"Those lies might work with the ladies, but don't even try 'em with me. We had a deal. No other women except Liza until after contract negotiations. You're not just blowing your chances with the Nats; other teams won't look at you either if you can't stay away from the parties and keep your pants on."

Cole clenched his teeth and stared at a hole in the worn backseat of the cab. Thoughts of Liza had kept him from going in to Nikki's party, but Frank would never believe that, especially after he'd pretty much called Cole a liar. "I've kept my end of the deal." Air hissed on the line and Cole imagined Frank taking a long drag of his cigar. He waited for the exhale, and it came a few seconds later.

"Say what you will, but it damn sure doesn't look like it. If you can't take your career seriously, then I sure as hell can't. I don't need your kind of trouble. I'm all set for money, son. And I've got a roster of top guys—more than I can handle. No need to waste my time negotiating for you. Either straighten up or find a new agent."

Cole sat there, blindsided, his heart hammering. Outside of his teammates and coaches, only three people meant anything to him—Mack and Brenda, and Frank. *And Liza?* How many of them was he willing to alienate?

"I understand," Cole said.

Frank cleared his throat, as if he'd been getting ready to say something but decided not to. "Then you and I are square. Now you need to figure out how to handle this with Liza."

Chapter Twelve

Liza sat at her desk on Thursday morning, preparing to go through the motions of making Frank's donation process look official. She'd asked him to come to the foundation today so Ross and her coworkers could see her making an honest effort at fund-raising.

An honest effort?

Okay, an *effort*—not necessarily an honest one. She certainly wasn't being honest with Cole, or maybe even with herself. If she were, she'd admit she wanted to talk with Frank about more than his donation. She'd woken up this morning to a heart-flipping tweet from Cole. Interested to find out what else he'd been up to, she'd clicked on his home feed and seen the stomach-clenching tweet from Nikki Barlow. Jealousy had bitten her and kept gnawing. No matter how hard she'd tried to shake it, she couldn't stop imagining them together and wondering what had gone on. Had Cole kissed Nikki the way he'd kissed her? She'd immediately called Frank, figuring his donation would be a sure thing now, so she might as well have him play the big-donor part.

Her office phone rang and she answered quickly. "Hi,

Carla," she said to the foundation's motherly receptionist, whose name appeared on the caller ID.

"Mr. Frank Price is here to see you."

"Thanks," Liza said. "I'll be out in a second."

She let Frank wait a little, hoping some of her coworkers would see him and start asking Carla questions. That would pave the path perfectly for his donation to look legit when it came in.

Just as Liza stood and smoothed her skirt, her phone pinged with a text message. She glanced at the text and her heart pitched. *Cole.* Twitter wasn't working out too well for him so he'd resorted to texting?

Wanna come to Philly tomorrow night? Baseball history in the making—division title on the line. Tix for you at Will Call.

No mention of the tweet from Nikki Barlow.

She let the message sit and went out to greet Frank under Carla's watchful gaze.

"Mr. Price," Liza said, "so nice of you to come."

Frank gave her an easy smile and stood. He had a cup of coffee in one hand, and shook her hand firmly with the other. "My pleasure, Miss Sutherland." He looked business casual dressed in black slacks and a mint-green oxford shirt.

"It's such a beautiful day, why don't we have our meeting in the courtyard, then I'll show you around?"

He followed her several steps, then turned back toward the receptionist. "Nice to meet you, Miss Carla." He tipped his cup to her and winked. "Thanks for the coffee."

Liza turned to see Carla blushing. *Like agent, like client.* Frank and Cole sure had a way with the women.

She led him out into the brick-walled courtyard to a wrought iron table and chairs nestled beneath one of the ginkgo trees. Ross and several of her coworkers had a view of the courtyard from their offices on the second and third floors. She hoped they'd all take notice of her meeting—especially Ross.

"Nice setup y'all have here," Frank said as they sat at the table. He glanced up at the back of the antique-brick townhouse and around the courtyard, his gaze resting on a cluster of mums. "Lots of orange."

Liza gave him a half smile. "Go Orioles."

He nodded, and things were awkwardly silent for a moment. "You want to talk about Cole?"

Liza was happy to bypass more small talk. "You saw his Twitter feed, right?"

Frank pursed his lips and nodded. "That starry sky one he sent you was pretty darn romantic."

"Not considering the tweet from Nikki Barlow that came after it." She lifted her chin, pretending this was all about business. "Cole is obviously seeing other women and not falling for me, as you claimed. So I'm hoping you'll consider making your donation to BADD immediately and release me from our agreement." Her heart thrummed. If Frank said yes, she'd keep her job and the camps would get even more funding from his donation. She could get back to her life as she'd known it—running the camps, following the Orioles, and missing Wes. Her comfort zone, as Paige would say.

But then you won't see Cole again.

"Are *you* falling for *him*?" Frank asked.

"No," she said, too quickly. "I just want your donation, and I want out."

"But that wasn't our agreement."

Liza picked up a yellow ginkgo leaf from the table and twirled it by the stem between her fingertips. "I realize that, and I don't know why I didn't think to add something like that to the deal. I mean, a guy like Cole was bound to go out with other girls."

"Why don't you give him a chance to explain that tweet from Nikki Barlow? Maybe it's not what you're thinking."

Liza's temper flared. "I don't care about Cole or Nikki Barlow or whatever is going on with them."

Frank nodded. "Whatever you say. Whether you do or not, our agreement stands as it is. If you want out now, just say. But I won't be making a donation to BADD."

Liza rubbed her forehead, thankful Frank was facing the building instead of her. Ross would really wonder what was going on if he could see her face. Her stomach felt hollow and she wished she'd eaten breakfast. On second thought, maybe not.

"So you've got a decision to make," Frank said. "Are you in or out? And if you say in, remember the terms. You date Cole until the end of the baseball season. And you can't be avoidin' him if he wants to explain that tweet, as I suspect he will." He slugged the last of his coffee. "No shenanigans."

Liza stared at the ginkgo leaf she continued to twirl as she considered her predicament. She needed Frank's donation—if she wanted to keep running the BADD camps and selecting deserving boys to attend, and if she wanted to prove herself without asking for help from her parents.

But she had to be honest with herself, too. She was definitely in danger of falling for Cole. Her jealousy over Nikki Barlow's tweet told her that much, and so did her heart. She had no idea how things were going to work out, but she couldn't give up now. She took a deep breath, released the leaf and watched it flutter to the ground. "I'm in."

Chapter Thirteen

Cole hadn't heard from Liza since he'd texted her yesterday. The Nats had the day off, and they'd traveled from Miami to Philly, giving him plenty of time to think about Frank's threat to drop him. Cole couldn't imagine losing Frank or working with another agent. Straightening things out with Liza would ease Frank's mind, and Cole's, too. Leave it to Nikki to complicate things just when he'd decided to take a real chance with Liza.

Cole needed her at tonight's game. It would show Frank that he had things under control, and it would show Cole that she was just as into him, too. Now he faced the game without her here, worrying what his next move should be. During batting practice, all the stress nagged at him, and he took it out on the baseballs. He smashed every one that came at him, and at least a quarter of them left the park. Feeling moderately better now that he'd knocked the crap out of something, he headed into the visitors' clubhouse with his teammates, ready for the big game. He sat in front of his locker, double-knotted the laces of his cleats, and checked his phone one last time.

His heart hitched. A text from Liza had come in just

minutes ago.

Good luck in the big game.

DVRing it? he typed quickly.

Nope. I'm in the stands.

Cole smiled and blew out a long breath. She was here.

He hated to admit it, but now he was twice as nervous as he'd been before he got her text. This was unfamiliar territory. On the rare occasion he'd invited a girl to watch him play, he came out with swagger, confident that whatever he did, she'd like it. But Liza was different. She knew the game. And it was going to take a triple and stealing home—the hardest play in baseball—to impress her.

See you afterward? he texted.

Only if you'll sing. ;)

No way. He smiled as he put his phone in his locker and joined the team on their way to the visitors' dugout. The night had gotten cooler quickly, and a fine mist made light in the stadium hazy. Rain was in the forecast, and Cole hoped it would hold off. Muddy baseball might be fun to watch, but it was definitely no fun to play.

When they stood for "The Star-Spangled Banner," he scanned the sold-out crowd and spotted Frank sitting with Mack and Brenda, and Liza—all Cole's VIP seats, all in a row. He calmed down a little. Things were okay for now, and he could worry about baseball. The Phillies had a way of sneaking up on the Nationals, and the Nats couldn't let that happen tonight. They were too close to clinching the division, and a win tonight would get it done.

Cole sat at one end of a ridiculously huge couch in the corner of the upscale hotel lobby, sulking. He wasn't dressed to impress in a pair of jeans and a worn Tar Heels T-shirt. But the clothes were comfortable and dry, and that was all he cared about right then. Nearby, an annoying wall fountain trickled water, reminding him of the incessant light rain that had ultimately soaked him during tonight's miserable game.

He thought he and his buddies would be celebrating clinching the division title. Instead, most of them had headed to their rooms, embarrassed and angry at themselves for letting the game get away. The Nats had taken the lead in the third, 2-0. Then a bad call at first had put the Phillies catcher on base. The next batter hit a homer, tying the game, and the Nats' momentum was gone. From then on, their bats were quiet, their bullpen struggled, their gloves were slippery, and they'd all-around sucked. The Phillies had won 5-2.

His phone pinged with a text from Frank.

Tough loss. Saw the little lady at the game. Nice work.

Cole needed to set Frank straight and tell him their plan had shifted. The only "work" Cole was doing with Liza now was trying to win her heart. He needed to make sure that wasn't complicated by a slip from Frank, clueing her in to their initial plan.

Seconds later, she came into the lobby, carrying a paper lunch bag. Cole stood and caught her attention. She made her way over to him, wearing a stylish black rain jacket over jeans and a snug ivory cable-knit sweater. The girl defined wholesome-hot. Two bellmen and a desk clerk checked her out appreciatively, and Cole had the knee-jerk instinct to take her in his arms to show those guys that she was his. Then he remembered that she wasn't...yet.

Even so, he pretended she was and hugged her tightly,

inhaling her flowery scent, and feeling better about the Nats' loss, if only for a moment. She wrapped her arms around him and it was the best feeling he'd had since he'd left her days ago.

"Hi there," he said, and reluctantly released her.

"Hi, yourself." She grimaced, yet still managed to look pretty. "You okay?"

He shrugged. "I've been better."

"I'm sorry about the game."

He clenched his jaw. "We'll get 'em tomorrow night." He sounded more confident than he felt. If he kept playing the way he had this week, he'd be no help to the Nats. Worrying about things between him and Liza and Frank had affected his game, but everything would get better now.

He led her over to the couch and they sat down.

"I need to tell you what happened between me and Nikki Barlow," he said quickly, before he lost his nerve.

She blushed. "I saw the tweet. But you don't really owe me an explanation." She bit her lip, looking vulnerable. Her reaction made him want to explain himself more.

"So the thing with Nikki..." His chest tightened. Saying everything he'd planned was going to be harder than he'd thought. "I had a bad game in Miami the other night." He shrugged. "Kinda like tonight. I was so coiled up inside— pissed at myself for making that error that cost us the game." He told Liza about Nikki's invitation, his bad decision to accept it, and that he'd taken a cab out to the party. Liza listened attentively, but only made eye contact with quick glances.

"I stood in front of the villa and debated whether to go in," he said. "But I didn't feel like partying, and I *really* didn't want to see Nikki again. So I left. She must've seen me outside, and that's why she sent the tweet. I swear I never saw her. I mean, I walked to the causeway and called a cab." He reached over and gently swept his fingers beneath her chin, guiding her head until she faced him. "Because I couldn't stop thinking about you."

She furrowed her brow for a quick moment, confusion in her eyes. "I don't understand."

He sighed. "There's something different about you. It's no secret that I've dated a lot of women, and the media have been more than happy to publicize that." He leaned close to her, his elbows propped on his knees, her hand in his. "But none of those women *know* me, including Nikki Barlow, and I'm not sure they really want to. They want my money, or my fame, or what they think is my glamorous lifestyle. But when it gets down to telling them I was the poor kid from Mebane, North Carolina, whose alcoholic mother was sure she was going to hit it big every time she spent our welfare money gambling in Atlantic City, I don't think they'd understand. And they wouldn't want to hear that my father wasn't around—whoever he was—and my mom was always in a bar, or off with her latest boyfriend. Or that my grandma raised me, scraping for every cent so I could play travel baseball and maybe land a scholarship."

Liza gazed at him intently.

"But you met me when I was an eighteen-year-old poor kid who was at baseball camp because of someone's charity. There you were, the Hall-of-Famer's daughter. You knew where I came from and what I was all about—but you liked me anyway." He could hardly believe what was coming out of his mouth, but he kept talking. "You were the first person who didn't seem to judge. Anywhere I went in my hometown, people knew me as the drunk lady's son."

Liza clutched his hand. "I'm sorry," she said sincerely. She hadn't lived that kind of life herself, but she'd worked with boys like him at the camps run by BADD. Maybe that was why she seemed to relate. *Or maybe that's just who she is.*

No wonder he was falling for her.

"So that's why I sent you the tweet about the stars and the freckles. And that I wished you were there…" He trailed his fingers down a lock of her silky hair. "That was all true."

She sat quietly for a moment, and he hoped she would say something soon. He'd gone and left himself vulnerable, and he didn't like the feeling. He was amazed how this girl who might not be that into him had made him wish she were.

"I brought you something," she said after way too long. She handed him the paper bag she'd brought with her.

He looked at her curiously, but she gave nothing away except her mouth quirking up at one corner. The bag crinkled as he opened it, and he pulled out a plain white napkin and a plastic bag. Inside it were four round sandwiches on white bread with peanut butter and jelly oozing out around the edges.

"Baseball PB and Js," she said.

Cole stared at the sandwiches, thinking that no one besides her had ever done something this thoughtful for him. Even after she'd seen Nikki's tweet and could've made all kinds of assumptions about what had gone on between them, she'd been thinking about his feelings instead of her own. Cole took her in his arms and held her tightly until a wolf-whistle pierced the silence. "Get a room."

Cole recognized his roommate's voice, and turned to see him heading for the elevators. "You're in mine," he teased.

He opened the plastic bag, pulled out two sandwiches, and offered one to Liza. She took it and they sat quietly, eating their PB and Js.

"Will these make me play better?" Liza licked some jelly from her lips and Cole got all kinds of ideas that had nothing to do with baseball or his grandma. He leaned over and kissed her softly, then rested his forehead against hers.

She leveled her green-eyed gaze on him. "Only if you believe they will."

If anyone could make him believe again, it was her.

He sat back and took another bite of his sandwich, thoughts of the game creeping back into his mind. He shook his head. "So much of baseball is mental."

"That's what my dad has always said."

Cole grimaced before he could stop himself. He was still really pissed about the game, and the last thing he wanted to hear was what Sutherland had always said.

Liza sat back and narrowed her eyes. "What's with you and my dad?"

She had to ask that question tonight of all nights. "What do you mean?" he asked, buying time.

"You seem to get tense whenever I mention him. And when you two were together at Sweet Bee's, something just seemed…off."

Cole leaned his head back on the couch and blew out a heavy breath. "I don't really want to involve you," he said gently, "in what's between your dad and me." He knew it was unrealistic, but he really did feel that way.

She gazed at him, her eyes looking darker in the dim light of the lobby. "So there is something."

Cole dragged his hand down his face. He had to get this out there if he expected to have any kind of real relationship with her. "Your dad was the best coach I'd ever had," he said. "I mean, he really knew the game, but he was even better at seeing guys' skills and playing them where they belonged. And he didn't put up with any crap from a bunch of cocky teenagers, either."

"I know." Liza nudged his shoulder. "I was one of them

once, too."

"I guess the short version of the story is that your dad was like the role model I never had. I really looked up to him. And your mom was so…motherly. Kind of like my grandma, but younger, obviously. I got the crazy idea that they were my adopted parents, sort of, as weird as that sounds."

She smiled knowingly.

"So there I was," he said, "with your mom being motherly and your dad paving the way for me to play at UNC. And once I was there, they'd come to my games sometimes and take me out to dinner. Before I graduated, they bought into the Orioles. I remember how excited they were."

"Me, too. It was a huge decision for them. My dad was so thrilled to be able to stay so close to baseball, and my mom started BADD so we'd still have the camps."

"Right before graduation, your folks and I were out to dinner one night." He remembered the exact booth they'd been sitting in at the Outback Steakhouse between Chapel Hill and Durham. "And your dad really built up my hopes about being drafted by the Orioles. He said there was some behind-the-scenes negotiating going on, and he was sure things would work out."

Liza drew her head back and lowered her eyebrows.

Cole pressed his lips together tightly. "But at the last minute, I was drafted by the Nationals."

"The draft is so unpredictable," she said. "My dad *always* wanted you to play for the Orioles, but he said the Nats snatched you up before the Os got their chance."

"That's what he told me afterward, too, but he'd been so certain about me going to the Orioles. I had my heart set on it." Even though Cole was successful now, he couldn't help but wonder what might have been if things had worked out with the Orioles—and with John and Sylvia. "It was a really awkward time. After that, we just drifted apart. I got a birthday card from them every year. A Christmas card, too, I think."

"They still talked about you a lot," Liza said, as if she thought he needed to hear that. "I figured you all were going in different directions with your teams, and just didn't have the time to get together anymore."

Cole shook his head, still feeling hollow from losing them. "They were like family…and then they were gone. I've always thought, when it came down to it, your dad changed his mind about me and the Orioles backed out of the deal. I can't blame anyone but myself, but I spent years playing in the minors and blowing chances at the top because my head was so screwed up."

Liza took his hand in both of hers. "I hate that that happened to you. But there has to be more to the story."

He tensed. "Not my side of it."

She raised her eyebrows. "Then it'll be interesting to hear what my parents have to say about theirs."

"I'd prefer you didn't ask them." He had spent all these years trying get past what had happened between him and her parents. He'd lived with his version of the story, too embarrassed and too proud—if that were possible—to try to make things right with them. But Liza was a make-things-right kind of girl, and if he was going to have a relationship with her, it would also have to include her parents. She didn't say anything, just met his eyes with a measured gaze that told him she would ask them anyway.

"So imagine my surprise," he said, "when I saw the tweet announcing you'd won the auction date."

She nodded slowly. "Imagine mine."

• • •

Liza's head was spinning with all of Cole's revelations. She sure hadn't expected his story about Nikki Barlow. It was hard for her to believe he'd given up partying with a movie starlet because he was thinking about her. But he'd made a convincing argument that had made sense and tugged at her heart. He was definitely making himself harder for her to resist.

"Are you going to stay and go to the game tomorrow?" Cole asked, looking hopeful.

She had planned to meet her parents in New York, where the Orioles were battling the Yankees for their division title. The Os had won tonight, but their fight was probably going to last until the bitter end. She'd like to go to New York—to confront her parents about what had happened with Cole—but now that he'd asked her to his game tomorrow, she'd much rather stay here. "I don't have a reservation," she said. "I was headed to New York to catch the Os games this weekend."

Cole lifted her hand and kissed the top of it. "I really wish you'd stay," he said, his tone a notch lower than usual. "I'll get you a room."

Liza's insides swirled. He was so incredibly tempting. "Me, or us?" She wasn't sure what she wanted his answer to be.

He absently swept his tongue across his bottom lip and she forced herself to look away. "Either."

The decision was hers. She started to debate with herself, but then decided not to overthink things. "Okay," she said. "But I'll get the room."

He smiled, kissed her on the cheek, and stood, pulling her to her feet. They went to the front desk and Liza checked in, excited and nervous and amazed that she was staying here with Cole.

The desk clerk handed Liza her key card. "Enjoy your

stay, Miss Sutherland."

"Thank you," Liza said, and looked shyly at Cole.

They got Liza's things from her car and went to the room. Cole called room service for some beers and nachos. They sat at the small table in the room and dug in.

"You sure know how to pick a midnight snack." Liza munched on a nacho and took a sip of beer. She was glad they could eat in privacy and enjoy watching ESPN.

"I do a mean breakfast, too." He grinned.

Heat crept up Liza's neck and into her face. It was a casual proposition, but one she wasn't quite ready for. "Even I can cook with room service."

She was thrilled to see the highlights of the Orioles' win over the Yankees, but she noticed an obvious change in Cole's mood when the analysts reviewed the Nats/Phillies game. He raked both hands through his hair and grasped the back of his head, frustration etched on his face.

"Tomorrow will be better," she said.

"And I need to be ready for it." He pushed his chair away from the table. "I need a good night's sleep and a clear head."

She quietly blew out a long breath. That was just the segue she needed to keep both of them from doing something she knew she'd regret. She tucked her chin and gazed at him demurely. "Then you'd better get going."

She stood and held her hand out to him, ready to walk him to the door. He grasped her hand, wrapped his muscular arm around her waist, and pulled her onto his lap.

• • •

Cole knew he shouldn't stay with her. With Liza in the bed, he'd never sleep. And whether it included something more or not, she wasn't ready to share a bed with him. But he couldn't leave her without a kiss.

She shifted in his lap, facing him, and his blood ran hot and rushed low. Her eyes widened and her lush lips parted. Unable to resist her any longer, he touched his lips to hers, channeling all of tonight's intense emotions into their kiss. She responded with sensuous sweeps of her tongue in perfect rhythm with his, her floral scent enticing him.

His body hummed as she combed her hands through his hair and pulled him toward her with a gentle rake of her fingernails against his scalp. A familiar pressure built inside him. Her movements on his lap tempted him to quickly carry her to the king-size bed, forget all caution, and claim insanity later. He traced his fingers beneath her sweater, just far enough to get his hands on the velvety-smooth skin at her waist, and pressed her down firmly as his hips rose.

He could hardly restrain himself. No matter how much he denied it, he was completely wrapped up in her—physically and emotionally. *And I'm going to make her mine.*

Just when he'd decided to barrel ahead without worrying about consequences, Liza broke off their kiss and brushed her nose across his. He inhaled sharply. This girl could even make Eskimo kisses hot.

Cole had to give her credit for having the discipline he lacked. He leaned his head back, took a deep breath, and willed away the pressure inside him that had tightened into a knot. Still clutching her waist, he circled his thumbs over the soft skin stretched over tight muscle. He risked moving his thumbs a little higher. She flinched and giggled.

"You're ticklish?" He lightened his touch and she laughed. Seeing her looking so carefree turned him on even more.

"No." She tried to pry his hands away, wriggling in his lap, torturing him with every move. He felt like a teenager again, fighting to keep himself from losing it.

Reluctantly, he pulled his hands away and raised them in surrender. "Okay, okay."

Still smiling, she pressed her palms and fingers to his, her hands looking delicate and small. "Tomorrow, the Nats will win. Then, we'll celebrate." She kissed him lightly, and stood.

Cole smiled and nodded. *That'll be some celebration.*

Chapter Fourteen

Liza slid the key card into the door of her hotel room in the early hours of Sunday morning. Cole lazily rested his hand at the back of her neck, and she liked his casual closeness. Blame it on the champagne, the celebrating, or the special attention he'd given her since the Nats won their division tonight, but something in her was changing.

Amid the partying, he'd proudly introduced her to his teammates and Nationals' executives—and endured all kinds of emasculating pie-baking jokes—as if he'd won her in the lottery. Maybe he thought he had. He'd been pretty open about being cautious of the women he'd dated and their motives. No doubt some of them had wanted him for his money and fame. Add that he was super sexy and nearly irresistible, and he didn't stand a chance—especially if he was looking for something *real*. It had simply been easier for him to keep things casual and keep the line moving. He'd seen his mother do that all of his life, and he'd learned from her example. Plus, he'd had no father to show him anything different.

Liza wasn't the only one with a comfort zone. Cole had stayed away from serious relationships for another reason, too. He hadn't trusted that anyone would stick around. His grandma had been there for him, but the three other people he'd needed most—his mother and Liza's parents—had left him on his own.

He seemed to have no idea that she, too, had a questionable motive for dating him. But could she really walk away from him when the time came? She might be the first woman who *left* him for money.

The idea made her feel guilty and cheap, even though the money was for a good cause. Her hazy thoughts circled back to her commitment to Wes, her need for Frank's donation, her desperation to prove herself at BADD without her mom's assistance, and her desire to keep the job she loved. Her growing attraction to Cole was totally outside her comfort zone. Giving in to it would mean sacrificing everything else. She wasn't ready to leap toward that decision just yet, but she was ready for baby steps.

"I'm glad you decided to stay another night," Cole said after they got in the room. His eyes were glassy with a champagne buzz, and she suspected hers were, too.

"Remember your end of the deal," she said. She hadn't needed his permission, but she felt more comfortable since he'd agreed that she could ask her parents about what came between them and Cole.

He sat at the foot of the bed, frowning. "I didn't want to dredge up all that."

The champagne had made her feel bold. She nudged herself between his legs, pushed him back onto the bed, and straddled him across his waist. "Then you shouldn't have taken up with me."

Her heart quickened at the sight of him lying beneath her, broad-shouldered and perfectly fit, his hair blonder against the ivory duvet, his eyes sparkling. She inhaled the heady scent of his blue cologne, tinged with champagne. He splayed his strong hands across her thighs and smoothed them up to her waist. "I'm glad I did."

Feathery sensations swirled through her and came out in goose bumps. She leaned down and kissed his full lips, languishing in the pure male feel of him beneath her. He pressed her closer, reviving long-lost sensations that she'd desperately missed. Despite their clothes, her breasts strained against the tightness of his pecs.

In one swift motion, he flipped her onto her back, propping himself on one elbow. He softly kissed his way up her neck and gently tugged her earlobe. Need pulsed through her and she arched beneath him. "Liza." His breath was hot against her ear. He threaded his fingers through her hair and pressed his body to hers, his desire unmistakable. "I want you," he whispered.

His words melted over her, making her dizzy with sensation and champagne. She gazed into his blue eyes.

He kissed her gently. "Are you ready for this?"

Right now she was. Afterward, she might regret it. But Cole felt so good. After all this time, he made her feel wanted again. "Not yet," she said.

He kissed her lightly, then lifted one eyebrow and gave her a lopsided grin. "Then there's hope."

Chapter Fifteen

Sunday brought a win each for the Nats and the Os. Afterward, Liza had been glad to come home, but the weekend away had changed her—so much that she couldn't concentrate at work on Monday. She stared out her office window, thinking of lying next to him while he slept, watching the rise and fall of his sculpted chest and abs. He had the body and peaceful face of an angel—with that sweet mole on his cheek and a halo of silky blond hair. The angel tattoo on his upper arm had been an appropriate choice.

With a little help from her, he'd stripped down to his boxer briefs before they went to bed. Luckily, his clothes had gone slowly, piece by piece. Her heart had already been running on high. She might not have survived seeing a body as hot and tight and well-assembled as his unveiled all at once. His tattoo had caught her attention, along with all of his other remarkable assets.

"Wow," she'd said. "That's beautiful."

He gave her a rueful smile. "I got it after my grandma died. I figure she's my guardian angel, and this reminds me she's always close."

Liza lightly smoothed her fingers over the tattoo, gazing at the delicate artwork. "I love it."

She hadn't thought she could sleep with him in her bed, but she'd surprised herself and dozed off anyway. When she woke up in the morning, she'd been snuggled next to him, his arm draped lazily across her.

For the first time, she hadn't felt guilty about betraying Wes. Instead, she wondered if he might have sent Cole to her himself. And if he had, she needed to give Cole a chance. After work, Liza hurried home to change, then headed to Camden Yards where the Os would get their turn at clinching their division title against the Red Sox.

Cole had understood when she'd explained why she wouldn't be at his game. She wanted to share the title-winning moment with her parents—if it happened. Even Frank might understand that if he was still keeping track of their deal. It was the first time she'd turned Cole down for a "date" when he'd asked, but that might not really matter anymore. She was getting closer and closer to the edge with him—almost ready to risk everything. She was even considering telling him about her deal with Frank. If she and Cole were going to have a real relationship, she needed to be completely honest with him.

Liza got to the ballpark a little late, right before the first pitch. She made her way to the Sutherlands' box suite, where a buzzing crowd of people looked forward to the high-stakes game.

Her mom saw her from across the suite and hurried over. She wore black slacks and a flowing black cardigan with an orange camisole under it. Liza's outfit wasn't much different— nice black jeans, a long-sleeved orange top, and a lightweight black scarf.

Her mom's hug felt tighter than usual, and a little longer. Liza hugged her back, grateful that she could depend on her mom, no matter what. Sure, sometimes her mom went overboard, but that was better than poor Cole had had it. Her mom took her hand and led her to a corner of the suite.

"How are things going with Cole, sweetie?" she asked, a hopeful look in her eyes.

Liza couldn't keep her full-wattage smile from lighting up her face.

"You're falling for him," her mom whispered, loud enough for Liza to hear over the chatter in the suite and the noise of the game outside.

Liza wasn't ready to admit that…yet. To herself or anyone else. She'd learned from real life, and from watching *The Bachelor*, how most whirlwind romances turn out. During the first weeks of college she'd had one herself that fizzled out as quickly as it sparked.

"I definitely have a crush on him again," Liza granted.

"A sleep-with-his-autographed-baseball-under-your-pillow crush?" her mom winked.

More like a sleep-with-him-next-to-me crush.

Liza rubbed her neck as if she had a crick in it. "I think I learned my lesson on that one." She furrowed her brow. "There's one thing about Cole that I'm wondering about."

"What's that?"

"He said that something happened between him and Dad"—she lifted one shoulder—"and you, too, I guess. Back when he got drafted by the Nats, and you all drifted apart afterward." She hadn't expected that asking a somewhat simple question would feel so complicated, or that her mom would look so hurt. "What happened?"

Her mom put her arm around Liza and pulled her close. "It's a big night for us tonight, sweetie." Her voice wavered. "So why don't we save this for a better time?"

Liza narrowed her eyes and nodded. Maybe there *was*

something to Cole's side of the story.

During the bottom of the second inning, Paige showed up. She was hardly through the door before Liza was at her side.

"I'm so glad you came," Liza said.

Paige unzipped her jacket and glanced around at the people in the suite. "Tired of making small talk with the big shots?"

"Sure am. But you never know who might surprise me and cough up a grand or two for BADD."

Paige grimaced. "How's that going? Made any headway with that big donor you mentioned?"

Liza sighed. "Not as well as I'd planned. The guy might still make the donation, but I'd say the chances are getting slimmer."

"My offer still stands," Paige said. "I'm selling those pies like hotcakes."

Liza groaned. "You did not just say that."

Paige raised her eyebrows and leveled her gaze on Liza. "So tell me about your sexy-sexy weekend with Cole."

She couldn't keep herself from blushing.

"Holy hotness, Batman," Paige said. "You *did* it with Cole Collins!"

"Shh. Somebody might hear you. I did sleep with him but—"

"Where the heck are those sports bloggers when you really have news?"

Liza's stomach dropped, even though she knew Paige was kidding. She could only imagine the headlines for *that* story. "You wouldn't."

"You're right. But it was worth seeing the look on your

face when you were thinking about what they would write." Paige smirked playfully.

"What I was saying is we actually slept."

Paige hung her head. "There's absolutely no freakin' hope for you, girlfriend. You had the Crush in your bed and all you did was sleep?"

"That's not all we did." Liza grinned. The roar of the crowd outside caught her attention. "Wanna grab some food and sit down?"

"Only if you promise to give me all the not-so-dirty details."

Liza rolled her eyes and laughed. She and Paige hit the buffet, and Liza went straight for the hot dogs. While she topped them with mustard and onions, she noticed her dad off in the corner, talking on the phone. He had a dammit-I-mean-business look on his face, one that Liza always tried to avoid having aimed at her.

Paige followed her line of vision. "Somebody's not happy."

"Yikes."

They grabbed a couple of beers and sat down. Liza told Paige about her weekend with Cole while they ate, and the Orioles extended their lead over the Red Sox, inning by inning. Paige listened intently, cracking irreverent jokes whenever she got an opening.

"I'm happy for you guys." Paige nudged Liza with her elbow. "I hope things will work out so Cole can introduce me to one of his friends. But now that I think about it, why wait?"

Paige didn't meet many single guys, and she kept busy at Sweet Bee's most of the time. "Not having any luck with the AARP crowd in Maple Creek?" Liza asked.

Paige scrunched her face and drank the last of her beer.

After the Red Sox batter struck out, Paige turned to Liza, her Precious Moments eyes looking serious for once. "I think

Wes would be happy for you."

"I hope so," Liza said. "I'm still working through that, but I'm getting there. I'm starting to believe I can keep Wes's memory close and still have feelings for Cole."

"Keep believing," Paige said as the Orioles scored another run and the crowd went crazy.

The score was 5-0 Orioles in the top of the ninth, and the Red Sox batters went two up, two down. Liza and Paige joined her parents in the suite where the atmosphere was electric, and watched the pitcher throw two quick strikes.

The crowd roared louder than Liza had ever heard it in Camden Yards. "Os, Os, Os."

The pitcher threw a nasty slider over the plate that left the batter fanning. Game over. The Orioles had won the division title.

Fireworks exploded into the sky as everyone cheered and whistled and celebrated. Prouder of the Os than ever before, Liza cheered too. It warmed her heart to see the team in a huge victory huddle on the diamond.

Her dad hugged her tightly. "We're going to the playoffs, Slugger!" He had tears in his eyes, and hers welled up, too.

She and Paige hugged each other, swaying quickly back and forth, and chanting, "Yay, yay, yay!"

The only person missing was Cole. Liza wished he were here to share the excitement with her and her parents, as she'd been there with him when the Nats had won their division.

"Champagne and Orioles pie for everyone!" her mom shouted, popping a cork.

Liza glanced over and saw Orioles pies lined up on the counter, pretty as a picture. She grinned at Paige. "At least you made 'em…not me."

Chapter Sixteen

Cole's A-game had returned, and he knew it was because of Liza. The Nats' pitching had been lights-out tonight, and they'd beaten the Mets in record time. One more regular-season game, then on to the playoffs. The Nats had played tough all year; now they'd be vying for a spot in the World Series. Cole had dreamed all his life about playing on a World Series team. Maybe his dream would come true.

As soon as he got the news about the Orioles clinching their division title, he tweeted Liza, wishing he could be there to party with her. He thought about calling, but knew from experience that it was pure bedlam in Baltimore right now.

Cole Collins @Cole Collins
Congrats to @LizaSutherland, her folks, and the Os. Well played.

Within moments, Liza responded.

Liza Sutherland @LizaSutherland
Missing you. We'll save some pie and champagne! Go Os! #worldseriesbound

She'd attached a picture of her and Paige, wearing Orioles caps and raising flutes of champagne. Liza proudly held an Orioles pie, her chin tipped up, a satisfied grin on her face. Light from the camera shone in her green eyes, and she looked…happy.

Cole's heart flipped. This was the first time she'd ever tweeted him. She'd put it out in public that she missed him. That's all it took for him to decide to head to Baltimore.

Showered but not shaven, he left the clubhouse, hoping to get to Liza before too late.

"Heck of a game."

Crap. Cole recognized Frank's voice behind him, and turned to see him leaning against the wall.

"Got a minute?" Frank asked.

Cole wasn't in the mood for Frank tonight. His threat to drop Cole as a client still stung. "I was headed up to Baltimore to celebrate with Liza." He figured Frank would already know why.

Frank put a beefy hand on Cole's shoulder, his brow furrowed. "I think that's gonna have to wait. There's something important we need to talk about tonight."

Cole sighed, but his annoyance quickly turned to fear. Was Frank quitting on him? "What?"

"How about we head over to your place?" Normal people could just go to a bar for a drink or pick a local restaurant. But he and Frank would get no privacy in public around here.

They made it to Cole's apartment pretty quickly, considering the huge after-game crowd—another change since the Nats had started winning. Cole remembered wondering if they'd ever fill their amazing stadium, and now they did it regularly.

"Want a drink?" Cole asked, thinking he needed one himself, but deciding against it. He'd had Frank over several times before, and he always kept a bottle of scotch handy for him.

Frank nodded.

Cole poured him a drink and they sat in the living area of Cole's apartment—basic leather couch, a recliner, a coffee table. A giant flat-screen TV on the wall. The place was more like a modified Residence Inn than a home, but it was convenient during the season.

Frank was as big as the recliner. Except for the thick middle, Cole guessed he looked about the same sitting in it. "Cole, son," Frank said then lowered his eyebrows. "I'm the guy who donated the money to send you to John's baseball camps. I'm the guy who put you two together, then watched from a ways away while y'all got close, like family." He took a gulp of scotch. "I was younger then. Made a lot of mistakes. The worst one was envy. So when I took you on as a client back in the day, and John came to me with his plans to bring you on with the Orioles…"

Cole remembered the first time he'd met Frank, after one of his home games at UNC. At the time, he hadn't been fazed by the big-shot agent's offer to represent him. Things had been going his way, and the future had looked so bright. What a mistake it had been to think his track to the big leagues would be smooth and fast.

"I offered John a deal with another player." Frank blinked several times quickly and took a deep breath that lifted his broad chest. "And I told him and Sylvia to get out of your life."

Cole's heart hammered. He shook his head and narrowed his eyes at Frank.

"Believe me, they fought me like heavyweights—"

"Why would you do that?" Cole had never heard the tone in his voice—there were so many emotions fighting in it.

"Because I'm your father," Frank said, "and I resented them acting like you were their boy."

Frank might as well have hit him in the head with a baseball bat.

He was too stunned to speak as he raced to put all the pieces into place. *All this time—all my life—I figured I didn't have a father who gave a damn. And Frank was right there?* Cole closed his eyes and put his head in his hands, letting the news sink in. No wonder Frank sometimes knew more about what was going on with him than he knew himself. *But why hasn't Frank told me he's my father?* He hadn't been willing to step up to the plate, so he should've left John and Sylvia alone. Then Cole would've at least had some kind of family.

His thoughts flashed back to seeing John and Sylvia for the first time in years at Sweet Bee's.

We've missed you. Sylvia's sincere-sounding words had stayed with him. And so had John's. *Good to see you, Cole. Heck of a season you've got going.* Pressure built in Cole's throat, and he swallowed against it.

Frank bent forward, set his drink on the coffee table, and propped his elbows on his knees. He stared at Cole straight-on. "I got selfish about everything, thinking I wanted you to myself to make up for all that lost time. You see, I didn't even know about you for years. I'd met your mom in a bar at a casino in Atlantic City, and I bought her a drink. Lookin' lovely and lonely, she told me her boyfriend had dumped her and left her there with no way home." He furrowed his brow. "She said the guy hit her from time to time, so it was no big loss."

Cole's chest tightened and heat rose in his face. He hated to hear that kind of thing about his mom—he was embarrassed enough about his dysfunctional background, and he had a feeling that was about to get worse.

Frank sat up, fussed with one of his fingernails, then rested his hands in his lap. "Turned out we were from the same area—give or take a few hours—so I offered to take her home the next day. She had nowhere to spend the night, so I invited her to stay with me."

Cole knew where this was going. He was living proof.

"It wasn't like you're probably thinkin'," Frank said. "My room had two beds. She slept in one, I slept in the other—as much as I could, considering I kept thinkin' I'd rather be over there with her."

Cole nodded numbly. Men were all the same.

"And man it was a long drive home—New Jersey to North Carolina and runnin' low on sleep." Frank rocked steadily in the recliner. "Plenty of time for her to tell me all about herself, about barely finishing high school and workin' at Piggly Wiggly. I wasn't too long out of college myself, then, working for the Carolina League."

Cole had a hard time imagining Frank as a twenty-something kid who wasn't running his own show. Ever since Cole had known him, he'd been a well-established, well-respected, independent agent.

"When we got near Mebane, I figured she was giving me directions to her house, but we ended up on an abandoned farm. She asked me to park the car in the rickety barn so we wouldn't get caught where we didn't belong." Frank looked away from Cole. "Then she showed me how much she appreciated the ride."

Cole had been relieved he hadn't been conceived in a casino hotel room, only to find out it happened in a car in a rickety abandoned barn. "What kind of car was it?" he asked.

Frank smiled a little. "A red eight-banger Ford Mustang."

At least there was that.

"She was a sweet girl, your mom." Frank looked wistful.

"I called her not too long after that and asked her out. But back then, long distance was farther than it seems today. She said she was back with the boyfriend, and he was finally treatin' her nice." He stopped rocking. "I never even knew she got pregnant till your grandma tracked me down after your mom died. I was so sorry to hear about the accident, but then to learn I had a son? Sure, I was skeptical, but the blood types added up. Your mom claimed you were mine, and all I had to do was look at a picture of you to see you were the spittin' image of my dad when he was a boy."

Cole's mind reeled. Frank hadn't known about him until after his mom had died? Cole took a deep breath and exhaled slowly, trying to stay calm despite his building tension. "What do you mean, my mom claimed I was yours?"

"After your mom died, your grandma found a diary where she'd written about me givin' her that ride from Atlantic City. She said no guy had ever done something so nice for her and not expected anything in return." Frank shook his head. "Guess that's why we ended up in the barn."

Cole felt a pang of sympathy for his mom, and regretted yet again the life she'd chosen. But this was about his father. "What kept you away once you found out about me?"

"I was married by then, and my wife was havin' nothing to do with another woman's teenage kid—especially since she couldn't have kids of her own."

Cole thought about that for a moment. He could have gone from being the drunk lady's son to being another woman's teenage kid. No wonder he was so messed up. "So you became the invisible dad. The anonymous donor who sent me to baseball camp."

Frank clenched his jaw. "I'm not proud of it, that's for sure, and I wish I'd done things differently. But I tried to help out your grandma and you as best I could."

Cole remembered how things had gotten a little better for them financially after his mom had died. No big change, just an extra pair of jeans for back-to-school and snacks in the pantry that they couldn't normally afford—that kind of thing.

"When you were finishin' up at UNC, your grandma died. I sure hated to see her go, for her sake and yours. The wife was the ex by then, so I figured it was my time to step up." Frank was quiet for a long while, rocking.

Cole took a deep breath and waited.

"That's when I blew it," Frank said finally. He grimaced. "My big fat ego saw John and Sylvia actin' like family to you, and instead of being glad you had them, I was jealous." He gripped the arms of the recliner. "So I called them off. Poor Sylvia was beside herself, and John made a hell of a fuss, but I stood my ground and told them *I* was your father, and I could handle you and your baseball business." He pressed his lips together tightly. "I had a good deal worked out for you with the Nationals…"

Cole's gut clenched.

"They were building their roster," Frank said. "And you were just the type of kid they were looking for to hit the big leagues quick."

"But that didn't happen." Cole said angrily. "Because I lost it." He rubbed his hand roughly over his scruffy cheek and closed his eyes for a moment, trying to control his temper. "I lost my confidence because I thought John decided he didn't want me to play for the Orioles. Grandma was gone, and Mom had always been gone—even before she died. Then John and Sylvia bailed on me. All I had was baseball, and I couldn't even make that work."

Frank nodded slowly. "I'm sorry." He bowed his head for a moment, then set his blue-eyed gaze on Cole.

Blue like mine…

"I promised John and Sylvia I'd tell you that you were my boy." Frank picked up his drink and took a slug.

"But that never happened," Cole said sharply.

"I chickened out," Frank said meekly. "There's no excuse except I was afraid."

Cole had never seen this side of Frank, and it confused him even more.

"I figured you'd hate me if I told you that you were my boy after all this time. You might not understand why I wasn't around when you were a kid." Frank shrugged weakly. "I never meant for things to work out this way. You make bad choices in life and you pay. In the beginning, I kept angling for the right time to tell you, and I just never found it." He shrugged as if his shoulders were way too heavy. "I guess I never really found the courage."

He took the last swallow of his scotch. "Poor John and Sylvia had no idea I hadn't kept my word until I saw them at the pie war. There they were, still torn up about what happened after all these years, and hoping to mend things."

Cole took a deep breath and blew it out loudly. "So what made you tell me now?"

"John called me tonight, breathin' fire. Evidently Liza was askin' about what happened between you and her folks. He said either I tell you, or he was going to, and you'd probably take it a lot better comin' from me."

Cole frantically tried to make sense of everything. The idea of John looking out for him went counter to everything he'd believed for years…just like the idea of Frank being his father. Questions occurred to him faster than he could possibly ask them. "What about Mack?" *My uncle…*

"Mack's a heck of a brother—a good man," Frank said sincerely. "Better man than I'll ever be. He's hated that all these years have gone by without me tellin' you. It's come between us, really. But he's just gone about his business with you and kinda given up on me. Not that I blame him. I mean, we're still cordial, but there's been a rift. Maybe we can work on that now."

Cole cocked his head. "And Liza? When you arranged for me to get involved with her, you had to know this would probably come out."

Frank nodded. "Maybe it was my way of lettin' fate handle my problems for me. I risked losin' you, but I figured that gal could make you happy, and you'd get John and Sylvia back."

"So this was never about my contract?"

The mention of business immediately animated Frank. "Oh, I didn't say that, son."

The familiar nickname took on new meaning for Cole. It occurred to him that he'd never heard Frank call anyone else "son" all these years, but it had never crossed Cole's mind that Frank meant it literally.

"You definitely needed to settle things down. The Nats are still makin' up their minds about you. Your game is golden, as long as you stay focused. But you need to keep things steady with Liza so they understand you're serious."

"I am serious." At least Cole was certain about that. At this point, there was nothing fake about their relationship for him.

"Keep that attitude," Frank said, "and you'll be fine." His eyes got misty and Cole saw his Adam's apple bob as he swallowed hard.

Cole clenched his teeth. He was fighting so many warring emotions that he didn't know what else to say to *his father*. He stood abruptly. "I'm gonna go for a drive, just lock up when you go." He nodded, convincing himself that leaving was the best thing to do. "Everything's out there now, so…"

He grabbed his keys and left. Being alone was what he

knew, and that's what he needed right now.

Cole drove his pickup in silence, both hands on the wheel. *Frank is my father...* The news had dazed and confused him. He never would've imagined he'd learn who his father was, and why John and Sylvia had drifted out of his life, all at the same time.

Why had Frank done this to him? And why hadn't he told Cole before? His anger coiled tighter with each question. His life could've been so different if Frank would've been there for him. He drew back his arm, struck the steering wheel with the palm of his hand, then balled it into a fist. *Ow!* Stupid move. Showing up tomorrow with a self-inflicted hand injury wouldn't help him get a new contract with the Nats. He needed to smash some baseballs, but that wasn't going to happen tonight.

He rolled down the window. The crisp autumn air whipped against his face and thrashed his hair. For all these years, he hadn't thought there could be an acceptable explanation for what John and Sylvia had done to him. Turned out there was. They clearly weren't blameless in all that had happened, but Frank said they wanted to make amends.

But what about Frank? It might take a long time for Cole to wrap his mind around the idea that Frank was his father and figure out how to handle it. He'd always thought of Frank as more than an agent—kind of a wise adviser who was around an awful lot. But how could he have known that all agents didn't act like that? Frank was the only one he'd ever had. And Frank had been there to glue Cole's world back together after the Orioles hadn't drafted him, for all the good it did. Then he'd recommended his brother Mack to work for

Cole...

Mack had kept Frank's secret all along, too, just like the Sutherlands. But Cole couldn't blame him. What would Mack have gained from revealing the truth? As it turned out, Cole was closer to Mack than he'd ever been to Frank. Probably because Frank had always been knotted up with his secret, and Mack just wanted to help.

There was so much to sort out. Frank was still Cole's agent, and that relationship wasn't going to change anytime soon—if ever. This was no time to make rash decisions, and right before contract negotiations was no time to be looking for another agent. Cole sped down the open country road, thinking about Frank's recent threat to leave him. Now he knew just how empty that threat had been.

It would take Cole a while to muddle through all that Frank had said. To sift through the anger and bitterness and could-have-beens. And it would take him a while to adjust. Would he ever see Frank as his father? He couldn't say right now. The harder question was whether he could ever forgive him. *All those years without a father. All those years without John and Sylvia. All those years alone.* He'd do best to look toward the future now. There'd been enough damage done by shutting people out, and he didn't want to go through that hurt again.

As painful as all this was, he never would've unraveled the mystery if Sylvia hadn't set him up with Liza, and Liza hadn't insisted on finding answers. He glanced over at the empty passenger seat and realized he wished she were there. Her genuine smile, her tender heart. Her sexy wholesomeness. He couldn't stop thinking about how she felt in his arms, with her lithe body pressed to his. Fiery and feminine, yet fragile. Still unable to let herself go.

Even so, she turned him on more than any woman he'd

ever been with. But his attraction was more than just physical. He'd reconnected with her in a way he'd never expected. The girl who'd really understood him years ago still *got* him today. She was smart and funny and giving. She'd grabbed his heart for good the second she whipped out those baseball PB and Js.

Sure, he'd started dating her because of Frank's plan, but it really hadn't been about that for him since early on. It had been all about Liza. He wasn't sure about everything that had happened tonight, but he was sure he wanted to be with her. He swung his truck over to the side of the road, stopped, and pulled out his phone. He snapped a picture of the empty passenger seat and attached it to a tweet.

Cole Collins @ColeCollins
@LizaSutherland Comfort zone = not so comfortable. Wish you were riding shotgun. #wantyouwithme

Cole got back on the road and headed to Baltimore.

Chapter Seventeen

Frank needn't have worried about Cole keeping things steady with Liza. After he'd learned Frank was his father, she was exactly the solace he'd needed. She'd been there for him that night—listening to every question and every doubt, and she'd promised to be there for him whenever he needed her. How had he lived without her in his life? *Lonely...that's how.*

He wanted to be with her every day, but that was impossible. His playoff schedule was crazy and his stress level was maxed out. Even so, she kept him grounded, focused, and confident.

They'd looked forward to celebrating their respective league championship wins together—if they happened—yet as it turned out, both the Orioles and the Nationals won on long-distance road trips. The logistics hadn't worked out for them to be together, and through the games and travel and practices, Cole missed her every minute. Even so, the thrill of winning, and their teams meeting in the World Series, made what little time they had together that much more ,exciting. They'd stolen a date here and there, but Cole had waited for the perfect day for what he had planned.

He and Liza had headed out to Maryland in the mid-afternoon, with her riding shotgun in his pickup.

"Where are we going?" she asked, her eyes glimmering.

"It's a surprise." His nerves had started to kick in a little.

"You're full of those," she quipped.

Liza had become livelier around him, and there were fewer times when he lost her to what he figured were moments of grief. He got the feeling that was the last thing holding her back from letting herself go and really giving him a chance.

"This one's kinda special," he said.

"Sounds exciting." She grinned, looking relaxed. But that changed when they crossed the city line of Davidsonville. She gazed at Cole as he drove, looking vulnerable all of a sudden. "Wes is buried here," she said softly.

He nodded and glanced at her sympathetically. "At Lakemont Memorial Gardens."

"Is that where you're taking me?"

"I'd like to," he said gently. "If you'll let me." He reached over, clutched her hand, and smiled ruefully. "You've been there for me through so much. From years ago up to right this second. I couldn't have made it through the tough time with Frank without you." He lightly kissed her hand. "Dealing with the past hurts, and now it's my turn to be here for you. Let's go see Wes together."

Liza bowed her head and cleared her throat, her hair falling around her face. "We won't need the GPS. I'll show you how to get there."

Cole hated to see her struggling with so much emotion, especially since he was the cause. He was feeling emotional, too, but they had to make this trip. It would be painful for her, and difficult for him, but he hoped they could move forward afterward.

"Take a right up there by the stone wall." Liza's voice

wavered.

At least the late afternoon was bright, the cloudless sky a flawless backdrop for the color-tinged leaves and autumn-green grass.

Cole made the turn into the memorial park. The setting was serene among the rolling hills, with beautiful trees, colorful shrubbery, and picturesque ponds with fountains. He'd rather be buried somewhere out in the country, somewhere a little less structured, but he'd be okay if he ended up in a peaceful place like this. It reminded him of the cemetery in North Carolina where his mom and grandma were buried.

"Park near that weeping willow over by the pond," Liza said.

He glanced at her and caught her biting her lip. She gazed toward the willow and took a deep breath.

Maybe this wasn't such a good idea after all. But now that they were here, he had to go through with his plan. Turning around might be easier, but it wouldn't be helpful to Liza.

He parked the truck and went around to open Liza's door. She stepped down, took his hand, and started walking slowly.

"Wait." Cole opened the back door, grabbed a large shopping bag, and pulled out a bouquet of flowers. He was no expert, and he'd had no idea how the arrangement he ordered from the florist would turn out, but this bouquet was exactly what he'd had in mind.

Liza gazed at the flowers and pressed her fingers to her lips. "You..." She gazed at him, her eyes brimming with tears. "You didn't have to do that."

Cole hugged her gently. "I wanted to."

"This looks like an Orioles bouquet."

"That's what I was hoping." He had remembered his grandma loving orange lilies, so he'd started with those, and then had them mixed with white roses. The florist had suggested adding bunches of berries that looked almost black. The combination had sounded kind of scary—and a lot like Halloween—but Cole had given it a chance and been surprised at how pretty it looked. Liza seemed to like them, and that's what mattered.

She tipped her head toward the big weeping willow, which bordered a pond with a carillon tower beyond. "Wes is over there." She led him to a marble bench beneath the tree where she sat with the bouquet in her lap, and gestured for Cole to sit next to her. Centered on the ground in front of them was an unassuming pewter plaque that read *Wesley Andrew Kelley. Beloved son, brother, fiancé, and friend.*

Cole's heart hitched when he read the word *fiancé.* Embossed on the metal, it made Wes's relationship with Liza even more real—memorialized forever.

"We thought about putting *hero* on there." She nodded toward the plaque, as if she'd heard his thoughts. And what a nightmare that would be if he dared to even think about how he'd ended up here with her in the first place. All because Frank wanted him to make it look like he was settling down so he could get a better contract. He felt like a fraud sitting here at Wes's grave. Now that Cole's intentions were pure, he was terrified she'd somehow find out they hadn't been in the beginning.

"I read up on Wes and found out more about what happened to him. *Hero* is the first word I would've used to describe him."

Her eyes widened. "You researched Wes? I mean, beyond finding out that he's buried here?"

Cole's stomach clenched. He couldn't read the tone of her voice or her expression. This situation—and a girl this complicated—was an entirely new ball game for him.

"He's such a meaningful part of your life," Cole said

carefully. "I wanted to know more about him. But I didn't want to ask you too much, since I imagine it's painful for you to talk about."

She shook her head. "Not as much as you might think. What hurts more is when people intentionally avoid talking about him because they're uncomfortable and afraid to hurt my feelings. When you lose someone you love, there's nothing more healing than to talk about it. But most people get that this-is-too-awkward look in their eyes when I mention Wes."

The willow branches swayed in the breeze. Cole thought about what she'd said and decided it might've been a good idea to come here after all.

"Believe it or not, I can relate." He traced his fingers over the cool, smooth marble bench. "Not to losing a fiancé, but when my grandma died…" He swallowed hard. This cemetery had affected him more than he'd thought it would. "She was all I had. And there was no one to talk to about her because, by then, it was just the two of us."

"I like hearing about your grandma. She sounds like an amazing person…who raised an amazing person." Liza smiled. "I wish I would've had the chance to meet her." She lifted the bouquet from her lap and inhaled deeply.

"As strange as it sounds," he said, "I wish I could've met Wes, too. I hope you'll tell me more about him, but from what I know so far, he managed to be all those things y'all put on that plaque *and* a hero."

She nodded. "But he was so unassuming about it all. That's why we decided he'd like it better if we let his memory speak for itself. He would never have wanted *hero* written on his grave."

Cole couldn't begin to compare himself to Wes Kelley. But he did see some of himself in what Liza had said. He didn't care if he was named All-Star or MVP. Sure, it was nice to be rewarded for his achievements, but when it came down to it, he just wanted to be a good baseball player and a good teammate.

And a good husband... Now that he'd found a woman he could trust, the thought didn't seem so far-fetched. Liza didn't want him for his money or his fame. She knew exactly who he was and where he'd come from, and here she was beside him.

"I understand that a part of your heart—a part of your life—is here with Wes," he said. "Always will be. There's no way we could be together until I showed you that." He steadied the bouquet in Liza's hand, tugged out a rose from the underside of it, and stood, facing Liza and Wes's plaque.

"Wes, man," he said. "I know this isn't the way you'd imagined things would work out...having to leave so soon. But you seem like the kind of guy who'd want to know that the people you love are going to be okay." Cole took a deep breath. He was choking up like he did during every home game when the Nationals saluted the wounded veterans and the fans waved their caps. That song "God Bless the USA" got him every time. But this was even harder. Especially since Liza was blinking back tears, too.

"So I can promise you this," he said. "I promise I'm not as good a man as you, but I'm working on it. I promise I'm not trying to take your place, because I know I never could. And I promise if Liza will let me, I'll do everything I can to make her as happy as you would if you'd have had the chance."

Cole bent down and placed the rose on Wes's plaque. As he stood, Liza joined him, a tear trickling down her cheek.

"Thank you," she whispered. After a moment, she knelt down, put the bouquet next to the rose, and traced her fingers over Wes's name.

Cole gave her all the time she needed, as well as a little space. He stood behind her, regaining his composure, watching the geese swim in the pond.

Liza stood, brushed bits of grass off the knees of her jeans, and clutched his hand. She gazed at him, her eyes intensely green and glistening. "I never expected…"

Cole waited for her to say more, but she didn't. Even so, he could pretty much guess the words that hadn't come. He hadn't expected this from himself, either. But Liza had managed to bring out the man he wanted to be. The man he knew he could be and had been all along—underneath it all—but he just hadn't had the courage to let free.

He'd finally found a place where he belonged…with Liza…and it felt a lot like home.

The carillon bells began ringing. Liza took a long last look at Wes's grave and turned to Cole. "I'm ready now."

• • •

Liza sifted through her emotions as they walked back to the truck hand in hand. Cole had sneaked in through the side door of her heart like an unexpected visitor, and he was settling in. She hadn't really known it, but she'd been waiting for him to come. He'd helped turn her grief into hope and made her believe she could find love again. Taking her to Wes's grave today had been the one last thing she needed from Cole so she could risk giving him a chance, no matter what she had to sacrifice. How many men would've had the courage to do what he had done, or the heart?

They got in the truck, and he drove slowly out of the cemetery. The sun sank low over the horizon, and the sky was striped with orange and brilliant pink. Liza took it as a sign that Wes was pleased that, despite the crooked path she'd taken to get there, she was finally happy.

"There's something in the console for you," Cole said

after they'd driven out of Davidsonville.

Liza narrowed her eyes at him and opened the console. Inside was a box filled with several stacks of personally autographed Cole Collins baseball cards.

"For the boys at your BADD camps," he said. "And an extra one for you. I even put a girlie little heart after my name." He winked and her heart did a backflip.

"I am so gonna tweet a picture of that."

He grinned. "It's definitely one of a kind."

"Thank you," she said with a twinge of sadness in her voice. She wondered who would give out those cards next year, since it probably wouldn't be her. "Those boys will be thrilled, even though they missed out on girlie little hearts." She smiled, amazed by his thoughtfulness. "I'd like it if you'd take me back to my place."

Cole nodded, seeming to understand her meaning.

Liza sat for a while in silence, thinking about all he had done for her. He'd been so open, and he deserved the same from her. That included the truth about her deal with Frank. She'd meant to tell him sooner, but he'd been dealing with the stress of the playoffs, and his relationship with Frank was on such tender footing. And now there were all the emotions associated with Wes. Even so, she'd find the right time. *Soon… I'll tell him soon.*

They made their way back to Baltimore, and to Liza's place. By then, a starry night sky had blanketed the harbor. They stood on the balcony, arm in arm, gazing at the view. Liza rested her head against his chest and he lightly traced his finger across her nose.

"A girl without freckles…" He bowed his head and gave her a play-along-with-me look.

"Is like a night without stars," she said, smiling. She never would've guessed he'd be such a romantic. And all for her.

"Thank you for making this day about me…and Wes," she said. "But it wouldn't be right if I didn't say…" She stood on her tiptoes and lightly brushed her lips across his, the slight scrape of his whiskers sending an excited shiver through her. "Congratulations." She kissed him again, more fully this time, wanting to lose herself in him…soon. "On winning the National League Championship."

He smoothed his fingers down her cheek and over her lips, briefly dipping the last one into her mouth. She nipped at it, and her insides fluttered. She was so ready to experience all of him.

"If I'd have known this was waiting for me," he said, "I would've made sure we won it a lot sooner. Pretty sweet win for the Orioles, too."

"Come see what we've got." She took his hand, led him inside, and into the kitchen. "I bought champagne." She opened the fridge and showed him the bottle. "We can drink it now." She skimmed her fingers down his shirt—his abs so ripped she could feel each one through the fabric—and traced them around the button of his jeans. "Or later."

He quickly closed the refrigerator door. "Hmm…" He clutched her waist, lifted her onto the island, and stepped between her knees. "Is there something else you'd rather do now?"

Liza had never seen his eyes that sultry shade or been as captivated by that blue scent. She clutched the back of his neck, kissing him again, warmth pulsing inside her and settling low. She knew well enough where this was leading, and now she was more than willing to go there with him.

"You seemed to like the view from the balcony," she said.

"Beautiful." He nodded, slowly blazing a trail of heat as he traced his fingers down her neck to the top button of her blouse.

"The view from my bedroom is pretty nice, too."

His perfect lips quirked up at one corner. Liza couldn't wait to have them on her...everywhere. She slid off the island and onto her feet, took his hand, and led him to her bedroom. The curtains were opened to the floor-to-ceiling, picture-window view of the harbor, and moonlight illuminated the room. Mesmerized again by the view, Cole stepped over to the window and stared out while she lit candles, making the atmosphere perfect.

Liza joined Cole and took his hand. She raised it and kissed the tender inside of his wrist, then pressed his palm over her swiftly beating heart.

"Are you nervous?" he asked.

"Very." She stood on tiptoes and lightly pressed her lips to his. "But I bet you can make me forget that."

He wrapped her in his arms and kissed her tenderly, easing her inhibitions with each wisp of his tongue.

"Let's leave the curtains open." He swept his fingers beneath her chin, urging her to meet his eyes. "So I can see you in the moonlight."

Liza trembled a little, anxious and excited and amazed that she was in this moment with Cole. She imagined what he would look like, too, with his sculpted All-Star body bathed in moonlight.

He cupped her face in his hands, and sensuously smoothed them down to the vee of her blouse. With skilled fingers, he opened the first button, then the second, following with a trail of kisses as he went. The heat of pent-up desire swirled through Liza. She arched herself against him, his name escaping her lips on a sigh.

He peeled her blouse away and held her at arm's length, drinking in the sight of her in her lacy lavender bra. The passion in his eyes melted away her self-consciousness. She tugged on the hem of his shirt. "Take this off for me."

He obliged, enticingly revealing each ripped ab and well-developed pec as he pulled his shirt over his head. His tousled hair gleamed in the candlelight.

Sweet Lord...

Cole glanced at the bed behind her, flexing as he tossed his shirt aside. He raised one eyebrow. "A king-size bed?"

Liza remembered all the nights it had felt so empty. She looked at him demurely. "I know, right? It's way too big for one person."

"But it looks just right for two." Cole swept her off of her feet, as if she were featherlight. He cradled her against his chest and walked over to the bed, kissing her with abandon. Liza quivered, responding to his intensity—the hardness of his body, the tenderness of his touch. She hadn't known how much she missed this, or how desperately she wanted Cole.

"Mmm," she murmured as he lowered her onto the bed. "I forgot how good this feels."

Cole sensuously smoothed his thumb across her bottom lip. "There's nothing I'd rather do than help you remember."

Chapter Eighteen

Cole had figured he would always be single, because he never dreamed he would find a girl like Liza. She was settled, but sassy and sexy and sometimes complicated. And she came with parents like John and Sylvia, who'd accepted him again as if nothing had ever come between them.

He'd seen them several times since the night Frank had revealed he was Cole's father, and they'd even made it to one of his league championship games. They'd picked up right where they'd left off years ago, making Cole feel like one of their own. Only now things were even better, with Liza at the center of it all. Poor Wes had really missed out, and given Cole the gift of a lifetime.

One Sunday, when they were all in town, Liza took him to the Sutherland family breakfast. Sylvia whipped up some mean French toast with crispy bacon. Cole gobbled it down, thinking how different things were since he'd ordered that Walk of Shame burrito at breakfast with Frank at Ted's Bulletin.

"I can't remember the last time I had a home-cooked breakfast." Cole rubbed his stomach. "Much less one so delicious." He smiled at Sylvia. "I forgot what a good cook you are." He grinned at Liza. "It's a shame that Liza can barely boil water."

She rolled her eyes, still managing to look beautiful. "I have other skills."

Yes, you do.

After breakfast, he and John went out on the back porch and kicked back in a couple of rocking chairs with their coffee. The trees in the wooded, rolling hills of their property were tinged with orange, yellow, and red, and the sky was electric blue.

It said a lot for his and John's healing relationship that they could sit without talking and be comfortable. Cole was thankful for that. Maybe one day he'd get there with Frank, too.

"I want you to know," John said after a while, "that none of what happened is on your shoulders. Sylvia and I should've done things differently, but it's easy to say that in hindsight."

Cole nodded. "I'm starting to understand." And he was, at least enough to say it truthfully. "All these years, I was angry because I figured you changed your mind and didn't want me to play for the Orioles."

John reached over, clutched his forearm, and looked at him ruefully. "I wanted you to play for me then, and I've wanted you every day since."

Pressure built in Cole's throat. He never thought he'd hear those words from John. "I appreciate that."

"Sylvia and I are proud of what you've accomplished, even though we've missed so much."

Liza had helped him see how John and Sylvia had suffered, too. They'd wanted Cole in their lives, but they'd also wanted him to finally have a father. Frank had made it clear that he didn't want them around, and the last thing they could bring themselves to do was come between him and his father. They'd been hurt, too. "I admit that I didn't understand... before," Cole said. Over the years, he'd imagined saying lots of things to John, but none of them had been very sportsmanlike. The truth had taken the edge off his temper, and Liza had softened it even more.

"We didn't either, son."

And there it was again. *Son.* After an entire life without a father, Cole had two men who called him that now, even if it was a figure of speech. He liked to think there was more to it than that.

"Liza seems happy," John said. "We've been so worried about her since Wes died." He furrowed his brow. "What a shock that was, to lose him...and her too, really, for a time. It's nice to see that sparkle back in her eyes."

Cole wondered if John saw the same sparkle in his, but it sounded too girlie to ask.

A flock of birds came into view, flying south. Cole was fascinated by their formation—how they kept adjusting into an almost-perfect vee.

Maybe his life was starting to line up like that, too.

"To the National League Champion Nationals." Liza toasted Cole with her longneck beer, amazed at how much she'd changed since their stilted first toast on their auction date.

"And to the American League Champion Orioles."

They'd had an easy time giving each other props at this stage, but it would get a lot harder when their teams faced each other in the World Series. There had been plenty of celebrations, but this one was just for the two of them. It had been days since they'd been able to steal some time together, much less nighttime. Cole had made the arrangements and texted her earlier today.

Let's go back to the storybook farm…

How could three little dots be so exciting? She couldn't wait to get back to the farm, and this time they'd be all alone.

She and Cole had headed straight to the pond, where the logs and kindling had already been laid for a fire.

"Some pretty decent friends Mack's got," Liza said as they spread out their blankets on the ground. The Adirondack chairs were still there—with their curly-W cushions—but she and Cole could get a lot closer on the blankets, sitting with their backs propped against a couple hay bales.

The end-of-October nights were chilly and crisp, and this one was especially starry.

"You nervous?" Liza asked, snuggling close to him.

"About the Series?"

"Unless there's something else to be nervous about," she teased.

"Are *you*?"

"Sure. My loyalties are split. I want it for you because you and the guys have worked so hard." She kissed him lightly and was tempted to linger, but she'd never finish what she wanted to say if she did. "And I want it for the Os, and for me and my parents. They've got so much of themselves invested in the team."

He frowned like a little kid, and she imagined him as a four-year-old, begging to stay up past his bedtime. "But the Nats have never won one."

She scrubbed her hand through his hair. "Now who's looking for the sympathy vote?"

The fire sizzled and popped, the flames dancing as if Jason Aldean were singing in the embers.

"You must be nervous, too," she said.

"Without a doubt." He shook his head. "Man, there were times I wondered if I'd ever get out of the minors." He sipped his beer, seeming amazed at how far he'd come. "Then, when I was finally called up and stayed, I wondered if the Nats would ever be a winning team. But somehow we got it together—like voodoo baseball magic or something—and here we are… headed for the World Series. Now that I have you, and things are squared away with your folks and Frank, my confidence is at a whole new level."

She smirked, trying not to laugh.

"What?"

"Did you just say voodoo baseball magic?"

His eyes sparkled in the firelight. "Yep."

She traced her finger from his earlobe, across his stubbly jawline and under his chin. "You believe in that?"

"Sure. There's always that elusive something that makes things click like they never have before. Maybe for you, it's fairy dust." He winked.

Liza rolled her eyes. "I wish I'd had buckets of fairy dust to sprinkle around over the years. Don't you?"

"I'd have probably used it to make a few changes. But looking back, I can see how most things happened for a reason, and I wouldn't have learned much by making it easier on myself. It sure sucked at the time, but I needed to play in the minor league—to get better…" He gave her an I'm-embarrassed-to-admit-this grin. "And to get my ego under control."

She gasped playfully. "You had an ego problem?"

He lowered his eyebrows. "Come on, it's been downsized." And there was that stomach-flipping grin again. "A little."

Liza kissed him, his sandpapery stubble tickling her lips. "I think you've managed to get it just right."

Just right. The words resonated in Liza's mind, but they were no longer attached to Wes alone. Things were definitely feeling just right with Cole now.

He tugged her into his lap, wrapped the blanket around them, and held her close. There was no place she would rather be right now, and no one else she would rather be with. Liza no longer cared about Frank's donation—she'd find other donors the honest way. The only thing that mattered was being with Cole.

"Good or bad, everything that's happened has gotten me to where I am right now." His voice was deep and husky. "Here with the woman I love."

Her heart skipped a beat, then took off racing. Cole loved her? He'd sounded confident and sure of it, giving her the certainty she needed. She wanted to tell him, too—right now—but he leaned in and gently kissed her. "So given the chance…" He rested his forehead against hers. "I wouldn't change a thing."

Liza swallowed against a rush of emotion. She had never expected to find love again, especially not with Cole. But here she was—finally all in—and eager to prove it to him. Her insides swirled with the heat and energy of the fire. She shifted herself off his lap and lay down, urging him to join her.

He tucked an extra blanket beneath her head and stretched out next to her, propped up on his elbow. She combed her fingers through his hair and kissed him once quickly. "I," she whispered and gave him a longer kiss. "Love," she said breathlessly. Passion built in their kiss, and she could barely get out the last words. "You, too."

Under a blanket of fleece and a sky full of stars, she showed him how much.

Chapter Nineteen

Cole thought he'd experienced every kind of baseball stress—with injuries and trade worries and performance anxiety. But none of those compared to the pressure he and the Nats had put on themselves going into the World Series.

Fortunately, the National League had won this year's All-Star game, giving the Nationals home-field advantage in the first game. The Nats had taken that one, then dropped the second to the Orioles. This Series was a big-time version of the long-standing "Battle of the Beltway" rivalry between the two teams, so the Nats had headed up I-95 to Baltimore for games three, four and five. Cole had hoped the Nats wouldn't need that many games to take the Series, but the Os weren't going down easy, and they'd led the Series three-two. He had to give John's team a lot of credit, but the Nats' sole focus right now was to crush them.

Back home at Nationals Park, the Nats had tied things up with an unexpected shutout, so tonight's game was it. Expectations were high, and so was tension. Cole had never been so excited and nervous at the same time. His heart was locked in overdrive, all his systems running full out.

Two of the biggest moments in his life could happen tonight.

He'd had little time to spend with Liza, and he'd longed to have her with him. She was a little stressed too, with her loyalties divided between teams. He understood, and hated that he was helpless to fix it. But tonight, one team would win and the other would lose. They would deal with that and move forward together, just as they'd dealt with everything else.

Both teams came out swinging, but the pitchers were on fire and the game went scoreless through five innings. In the bottom of the sixth, the Nats' leadoff man hit a single. Batting next, Cole took the lefty pitcher deep into the count, and managed to tattoo a triple into the right-field corner. The crowd went crazy and the leadoff runner scored. Cole took third standing, his heart beating faster than the heater he'd just hit. The Nats had a heck of a record of winning when they scored first, and that RBI had just put them on the board in the final game of the World Series. But one run was no insurance against any team, much less the Orioles. The Nats needed to score a few more, lots if they could.

The following two batters struck out—one looking, one swinging. With two outs, Cole's scoring opportunities looked a little bleaker, but he always had hope when it came to the Nats. The next batter reached first by chopping one to the shortstop and beating the throw, but the play stranded Cole at third. He'd never been so amped, knowing what was at stake, and knowing that the seventh-inning stretch was staring him in the face after this inning. He couldn't undo what he had planned—and he didn't want to—but he couldn't recall ever experiencing such a sustained adrenaline rush.

His right-handed buddy came up to bat, and Cole watched carefully as he took a ball and a strike from the slow-windup pitcher. Before the next toss, Cole got a decent lead.

Distracted by the runner at first, the pitcher made his move to pick him off. Before the ball left his hand, Cole put his head down and tore toward home. He knew there'd be a play at the plate, and he knew it would be close.

As if in slow motion, Cole hit the ground, sliding headfirst at the bag as the ball streaked toward the catcher. The throw curved offline and the catcher shifted away from the plate to make the grab.

"Safe!" the umpire yelled, dramatically crossing and uncrossing his hands.

The crowd went ballistic, and shouts of "Crush, Crush, Crush" echoed through the stadium.

Cole jumped to his feet. He kissed his index finger, raised it high in a number-one sign and pointed straight to Liza.

He'd stolen home for her.

She cheered, even though Cole's run had just put the Nats up 2-0. The guys in the dugout were on their feet, too, and they met him with back-slaps, low-fives, and fist bumps for making the hardest play in baseball in the final game of the World Series.

A fly ball to center field ended the sixth, and they were into the seventh-inning stretch. But this seventh-inning stretch was different from any of his career. Cole dashed to his locker in the clubhouse, opened the safe, and took out the box of Cracker Jack he'd put there before the game. He headed up through the tunnel and out toward home plate, amid questioning glances from his teammates gathered in the dugout.

The seventh-inning stretch at Nats Park always started with the crowd singing "Take Me Out to the Ball Game." But tonight's version was going to be a little different.

Cole stood at the plate that he'd slid into just minutes ago, hoping to make an even bigger play.

"Ladies and gentlemen," the announcer's voice boomed. "Please direct your attention to home plate and the scoreboard screen for Nationals All-Star first baseman Cole Collins."

The crowd cheered and booed, depending on which team they were rooting for, but that was just background noise to Cole. All he could hear was his pulse pounding in his ears. A sound guy scrambled around behind him. He took a deep breath as the announcer continued.

"Joining Cole is Miss Liza Sutherland."

John escorted Liza to the plate. She looked blindsided but beautiful, with the night breeze catching her hair and color rising in her face.

The crowd clapped and whistled, then became surprisingly quiet.

John nodded at Cole, smiling, and stepped away. Cole took Liza's hand and gripped tightly to keep his own from shaking.

"Tonight's lyrics for 'Take Me Out to the Ball Game' have been revised for this special occasion and can be found up on the scoreboard," the announcer said. "Ladies and gentlemen, please sing along."

The organist played a few chords, and the crowd broke into song along with Cole, who was thankful everyone else drowned him out. What a time to debut his lack of singing talent to Liza.

Here we are at the big game,
Right in front of the crowd.
I bought you a ring and some Cracker Jack,
We've come so far we can never look back.
So I've got a question to ask you,
If you say no it's a shame.
Liza, will you…marry…me…please!
We'll play life's…ball…game.

The crowd roared as Cole got down on one knee, then became mostly quiet with a random whistle here and there.

"Liza," he said. Her name reverberated through the stadium, and he wondered how the hell he was going to get through this. It seemed like a good idea before his voice was amplified for over forty thousand people to hear, and all eyes were on him for a reason other than baseball. Shouldn't he have done this at the farm? He'd thought of that but decided against it. He wanted Liza to know that this was forty-thousand-witnesses serious to him.

"I guess that was pretty cheesy," he said.

The crowd laughed and cheered.

"We've kinda been through this before, but that was just for practice." He winked at Liza and sucked in a deep breath. His heart thudded so loudly he figured the mic was probably picking up the noise. "But this time it's for real." Cole pulled the ring from the Cracker Jack box and it sparkled under the stadium lights. "I love you, Liza. Will you marry me?"

The crowd became way too quiet as Cole stared into Liza's eyes, waiting.

She gave him the most gorgeous smile he'd ever seen and said, "Yes."

The crowd went wild as Cole slipped the ring on Liza's trembling finger. He got to his feet, took her in his arms, and kissed her.

While he'd been working at stealing home, she had quietly stolen his heart.

• • •

If it were possible to burst from excitement, Liza figured it was about to happen to her. She couldn't believe *she* was the larger-than-life girl up on the scoreboard who'd just gotten engaged to Cole. *Engaged to Cole! In front of all these people!*

She hadn't hesitated to say yes. Despite what had happened to Wes, and her fear that something similar could happen again, she'd instantly agreed to take a risk with Cole. She had no doubt that her heart belonged to him.

The crowd still cheered as Cole—looking wicked baseball-sexy in his uniform and cleats—led her over to the Nats' dugout, her legs a little wobbly. His teammates rushed them, huddling around and showering them with buckets of bubble gum. Liza finally knew firsthand how exhilarating it was to be in the middle of one of their celebrations. This one was hers, too.

As the guys headed back to the dugout, she said to Cole, "You've amazed me twice tonight."

He drew his head back and grinned. "Just twice?"

She laughed, her smile lingering. "You stole home."

"Just for you."

She cocked her head. "And a little bit for the Nats?" She smoothed her fingers down his muscular arm and squeezed his hand. "I'm willing to share you, just this once."

He raised one eyebrow. "Oh, you are?"

The teams headed out onto the field, and Liza had to let him go. She gestured for him to lean down and she cupped her hand around his ear to make sure he'd hear her. "I hope you win."

Cole stood straight and kissed her lightly amid more cheers from the crowd. His lopsided grin melted her heart. "I already did."

• • •

Cole was so amped that his proposal had been a hit with Liza and she'd agreed to marry him. She was going to be his *wife*!

He used to think of that word as strictly four-letter. Now he couldn't wait for Liza to become officially his.

But there was a World Series at stake, and he was ready to make it two-for-two and lead the Nats to victory. But the Orioles didn't make it easy. They answered with two runs in the top of the eighth, and the Nats went scoreless in the bottom. Cole hadn't envisioned going into the ninth tied 2-2, but here they were. He kept taking deep breaths to settle his nerves, and his teeth were sore from chewing so hard on his bubble gum.

The Orioles went two-up, two-down in the top of the ninth, but their third batter took advantage of a mistake by the closing pitcher and slammed one into the center-field stands, giving the Os a 3-2 lead. The next batter popped the ball to the shortstop and the inning was over.

Cole hadn't lost hope, because he had faith in his team. He was batting fourth this inning, so hopefully he'd get a chance to score. All they needed was one to tie, two to win.

The Nats' first two batters struck out swinging. After two nerve-racking close-call strikes, the second batter tagged a blooper for a single, giving the Nats a lifeline. With the tying run on base, Cole came to bat, adrenaline pumping.

World Series on the line… Team counting on me…

A wicked curveball fooled him and he fanned it.

The crowd was on their feet chanting, "Crush, Crush, Crush."

But the umpire called another close strike that Cole would swear was low in the zone.

One more strike.

Cole took his stance. He and the pitcher stared each other down, the noise in the stadium deafening. First the windup, then the pitch.

The second the fastball was released, he knew the pitcher

had made a mistake. It torpedoed over the center of the plate, in the middle of the zone, and Cole scorched it off the screws. As soon as it left his bat, bedlam erupted in the stadium, and Cole knew the Nats had won.

Chapter Twenty

Dizzy with mixed emotions, Liza got ready to leave the box suite her parents had rented for the Series. Everyone there was still stunned by the Orioles' shocking loss. She hugged John and Sylvia good-bye, her heart heavy for them, and for herself. Then she and Paige walked to the door.

"You know that voodoo baseball magic you said Cole believes in?" Paige asked glumly.

Liza nodded. She'd told Paige almost every detail about the night Cole had first said he loved her.

"Well, it must work. I mean, this was totally his night. I'm sorry the Os lost." Paige grabbed Liza's hand and had a long look at her engagement ring. "But that was one wicked-romantic proposal."

Liza grinned. "It was, wasn't it?"

Paige's eyes welled with tears.

"Oh, sweetie." Liza hugged her tightly. "It'll happen for you soon, too."

Paige pulled away and sniffled. "I'm not sad-crying for me, silly. I'm happy-crying for you."

The atmosphere changed the second Liza left the suite.

There was a big-time party rocking in the stadium. This was the Nationals' first World Series win, and their fans reveled in the ultimate celebration. Liza was thrilled for Cole and his team, yet totally bummed for herself, her folks, and the Orioles. She'd never experienced so much excitement and disappointment within an hour's time.

I'm engaged to Cole.

She still couldn't believe his fairy-tale proposal, but the big, sparkly diamond on her finger proved it was real. Her hands were still shaky, but her heart soared, thinking about a future with him. She wouldn't get Frank's donation, and she might soon lose the job she loved, but she had Cole, and things would work out somehow.

She'd wanted to give Cole time to celebrate with his team, talk to the media, and do whatever it was that World Series MVPs do afterward, so she'd been surprised to get a text from him less than an hour since the end of the game.

Meet me in the Nats' family room. Love, Your Fiancé.

She replied: *On my way!*

Liza wished she could've thought of something clever, but she was lucky to get three words typed considering her trembling fingers. Moments later, her phone chirped, and she checked the tweet.

Cole Collins @ColeCollins
@LizaSutherland said YES! #marryme

He'd attached a picture of them at home plate, him on one knee. Liza thought her heart might burst. Oblivious to the crowd, she practically floated toward the home side of the stadium. Several people recognized her from the proposal and congratulated her as they passed. Some just pointed and stared.

Just before she made it to the secure clubhouse area, a fifty-something brunette woman dressed in full Nationals regalia—including a Cole Collins jersey—clutched Liza's arm and pulled her aside. Liza's eyes widened.

"I just want to tell you," the woman said, "you're the luckiest girl alive."

Liza grinned. "I am, aren't I?"

The woman nudged Liza with her elbow. "I just love Cole," she said, as if she'd known him personally for years. "You give that handsome boy a kiss for me, will ya?"

Liza smiled graciously, imagining this might happen from time to time. "Yes, ma'am." *Gladly.*

The corridor leading to the clubhouse and family room was strangely quiet, considering the home team had just won the World Series. But she was sure the party was happening close by—with hootin' and hollerin' and spraying champagne in a huge room covered in plastic. She hurried toward her own celebration with Cole.

Liza neared the family room, but before she rounded the doorway, she heard Frank's voice coming from inside, and then Cole's. Her heart hammered. He was going to be her *husband*, and Frank would be her father-in-law.

She stopped outside the door, in case they were having a meaningful father-son moment. They needed times like this to bond. She couldn't wait to see Cole, but she had the rest of her life to be with him, and their relationship was solid. Sacrificing a little time to Frank was the least she could do.

"...and I couldn't believe you stole home," Frank said. "Hell of a play."

Liza leaned against the wall, imagining how much it must mean to Cole for Frank to be so thrilled with him. What athlete wouldn't want to impress his agent...and his father?

"MVP," Frank said.

Liza heard what sounded like a slap on the back, but she couldn't be sure.

"It's pretty surreal," Cole said. Liza loved how humble he'd become.

"Between what you've done in the Series," Frank said, "and what you've done with Liza, you can be pretty darn sure the Nats are gonna offer you a new contract."

"You think so?" Cole asked.

Liza furrowed her brow and inched closer to the doorway.

"You made it look like you were settling down all right, but I never expected you to ice the cake with that proposal during the seventh-inning stretch," Frank said. "I'm surprised they're not in here wavin' a new contract at you right this second."

Liza's stomach knotted.

"And the little lady will never know your relationship had anything to do with you getting a sweet new deal," Frank said.

Heat radiated in Liza's face with the thundering pulse of her heart. She stepped slowly into the doorway, her legs rubbery.

Frank stood with his back to Liza, but Cole faced her. He sat casually on the arm of a leather chair, still wearing his uniform, soaking wet. She could smell the champagne all the way across the room. He stood quickly when he saw her, and his eyes flashed with panic.

Liza swallowed hard.

"What?" Frank shook his head and turned to see what had caught Cole's attention.

"How long have you been standing out there?" Cole asked her nervously.

Liza moved closer to them, hurt and reeling, and said quietly to Cole, "Long enough to hear that you used me to get a contract." Pressure built in her throat. "Long enough to know that everything you said to me and everything you did was completely fake." Tears burned her eyes. She shrugged weakly. "You're just an MVP liar, because you definitely had me convinced." A tear slid down her cheek and she angrily swiped it away.

Cole tried to take her hand, but she stepped beyond his reach. He winced. "Liza, I—"

"Don't even try to spin it anymore. I should've gone with my gut instincts about you because, you know what? They were right."

"It's not what you're thinking," Cole said gently, looking at Frank for agreement.

"As if having *him* back you up is going to help." Liza cut her eyes at Frank.

"I think we can talk this thing through." Frank nodded unconvincingly. "There's just been a little confusion."

Liza tugged the engagement ring off her finger, grabbed Cole's wrist, and dropped the ring in his hand. Her heart broke, thinking that was the last time she would touch him. But he wasn't *her* Cole, anyway. The guy standing there was the real Cole. Her Cole had simply been an illusion.

"Here's your ring back," she said. "You've done enough damage, so leave me alone. There shouldn't be anything confusing about that."

"But—" Cole said.

Liza held up her hand, refusing to listen to another lying word. She couldn't stand to be in the room with him and Frank another second. She was about to lose it, and she wanted to be far away from them when she did. She made it to the door, then turned and glared at Frank. "You can send your check to the foundation. Because I didn't fall for Cole. I was lying, too." She shook her head. "That was a half-million-dollar sucker deal."

She walked out the door and left her future behind.

• • •

Cole stared at the door, hoping Liza would come back, but knowing she wouldn't. At least he wouldn't if he were her.

He sank back onto the arm of the chair and dragged his hand down his face. The Nats had won the World Series—the World Series!—and he was MVP. Liza had agreed to marry him, and all the stars had lined up straight.

But taking Liza out of that mix diluted the excitement of the rest. How could he celebrate anything when he'd just lost everything?

"I'm sorry, son." Frank stood with his hands in his pockets, a pinched expression on his face. "I shoulda watched my mouth there."

Cole shook his head. Frank was right, but Cole couldn't shove all the blame on him. He should've made it clearer to Frank that he'd fallen for Liza along the way, and that his pursuit of a contract with the Nats was a totally separate thing. He figured Frank had seen that, but they'd gotten so sidetracked with the father issue… Hadn't it been obvious that he was in love with her?

"What was that about a half-million-dollar sucker deal?"

Frank lumbered over and sat in the chair opposite Cole. "I've been in the business of matchin' players and teams for many years, and I know a good match when I see one." He cocked his head and shrugged. "Now they don't always work out—for all kinds of reasons—but that doesn't mean the chemistry wasn't there. Lots of 'em do, though."

"Are you getting to the deal part?" Cole's patience thinned. How could everything have gone so wrong so fast?

Frank scowled, as he'd done many times over the years when Cole had gotten snippy with him. "After that proposal stunt on your first date with Liza, you called me and said we needed a plan B."

Cole's gut twisted, thinking about how shallow he'd been.

"But I knew a little bit about Liza and her folks," Frank said sheepishly, "as you've found out. Salt-of-the-earth kind of people. I was sure you two kids would make a fine pair. And I guess part of me wanted to make it up to John and Sylvia…and to you. I figured you datin' Liza might be just the thing that got y'all back together after all these years." He rubbed his forehead and frowned. "After all my mistakes."

"So you made some kind of deal with Liza?"

Frank nodded slowly, frowning. "She didn't trust me when I told her you were falling for her."

"I guess not, considering what she knew about me at the time."

"But I knew better," Frank said confidently. "So I told her I'd give her a half-million dollars if she dated you for the rest of the season and didn't fall for you."

Cole blinked several times. "What? You were going to pay her a half-million dollars if she *didn't* fall for me?"

Frank nodded. "She thought it would be easy money since she was tied up with her memories and all—really a sad situation. Plus, she wasn't too keen on your reputation with the ladies."

Cole understood, to a point. But the idea that she would take Frank's money now made his stomach turn. It just didn't seem like something Liza would do, and it was hard for him to believe his judgment of her had been that far off. "So she's expecting you to pay her a half-mil now?"

"No, not her," Frank said. "She wouldn't take the deal for herself—and it took a hell of a lot to get her to agree to it at all. The money goes to the foundation, so those needy boys can go to baseball camp."

Now Cole felt guilty for even thinking she'd made the deal for money for herself. The Liza he knew would never do that. She'd had nothing to personally gain from going out with him. Her heart had been with Wes, and there'd been no reason for her to believe Cole was falling for her, outside of Frank's hype. Cole's reputation had ensured that.

He still didn't like the idea that Frank had meddled, and that Liza had dated him because of a deal. But he *had* fallen for her and been lucky enough to win her heart—only to crush it to bits. His own heart broke, thinking about the pain he'd caused her. Pain she'd tried to protect herself from and certainly didn't deserve. He couldn't believe things had worked out like this. He'd finally found a home with her—and John and Sylvia—but now he'd lost them, again.

The only hope he had was to make Liza believe he loved her despite the path he'd taken there, and that he couldn't live without her now.

Cole slid the engagement ring onto the end of his pinkie finger and twisted it around slowly. "I love her, Frank." He shrugged one shoulder and made a sweeping gesture around the Nats' blessedly empty family room. "None of this baseball stuff means anything to me without her."

"Whoa," Frank said. "Let's not get carried away on emotion. You've worked hard to get where you are with this team. You deserve to be a World Series MVP, and you deserve a helluva new contract. Give it a little time, and I betcha this thing with Liza will work out."

There was only one way Cole could think of to make that happen, but he wasn't going to risk telling Frank about it. He had some media people he'd promised to talk to, and some celebrating to do with his team—whether he felt like it or not.

. . .

Liza didn't tell Paige what had happened. She didn't tell her parents or anyone else. She let them all think she was blissfully celebrating with Cole. A World Series win, an MVP award, their engagement. What a night it could've been.

But it wasn't.

Instead, she'd gone home, blocked Cole's number from her phone, then turned it off and sat on her balcony for hours, staring out at the harbor. Although the hurt was different, it reminded her of the many nights she'd spent in the exact same spot, grieving for Wes. It had gotten pretty chilly during the wee hours—even with a blanket thrown over her—but feeling cold beat feeling numb. How could she have been naive enough to fall in love with Cole? And to think Frank had been willing to donate a half-million dollars to BADD if she *didn't*.

After getting a few hours of fitful sleep, she woke up to a gray morning with steady rain.

How appropriate.

Thank goodness she'd taken a vacation day, having planned to be with Cole no matter what the outcome of the World Series had been. She could spend the day alone, but she'd learned from grieving where too much alone-time could lead, and she didn't want to go there again. Paige was the one person who wouldn't ask too many questions or judge Liza for being so stupid.

So. Stupid.

Liza powered up her phone and texted Paige.

Coming by this morning. See you then…

She slogged through the motions of showering and getting dressed in her most comfortable jeans, a long-sleeved tee, and a cozy, soft-yarn sweater that always felt like a hug. No doubt she could use one of those today.

She got to Sweet Bee's around nine, both happy and sad

to see that business was slow. Jingly bells rang on the door as she opened it.

Paige caught sight of her from the kitchen. She came out grinning, waving a section of newspaper, appearing tiny in her big white apron. "Look who's in the paper again!" She gave Liza a once-over and lowered her eyebrows. "Where's Cole?"

Liza shook her head, her bottom lip quivering, tears threatening to fall.

Paige furrowed her brow and rushed Liza into the kitchen, tossing the newspaper onto a stainless steel table. "What happened?"

Liza grabbed the newspaper. On the front page of the *Washington Post*, above the fold, was a shot of her and Cole, him on one knee, putting that gorgeous ring on her finger. Liza had looked in the mirror countless times in her life and never seen herself so happy. Tears blurred her vision as she read the headline.

"Perfect Play: Collins Gets the Girl."

Liza couldn't help but read some of the article.

"Prior to clinching the World Series with a two-run homer, Nationals first baseman and Series MVP Cole Collins hit a run-scoring triple, then defied the odds and stole home. He's also been busy stealing the heart of Liza Sutherland, to whom he proposed marriage during the seventh-inning stretch…"

Paige grabbed Liza's hand. "Where's your ring?"

With plenty of tears and tissues, Liza told Paige what had happened—including her deal with Frank. Paige hugged her, way better than a sweater. She didn't judge her for being so drawn in by Cole or for agreeing to such a sleazy deal.

"He had me convinced, too." Paige shook her head.

"It was a pretty clever plan, and I fell right into it. With the press showing up at the farm that first night—"

"And me," Paige said, "stupidly letting him come here for

the pie war." She scrunched her face.

Liza smiled wanly. "At least you got some business out of this embarrassing mess."

"You don't have anything to be embarrassed about. I would've fallen for his charm a heck of a lot faster than you did."

Liza blotted her eyes, glad she hadn't bothered with mascara. "He used me as a tool in front of forty-one thousand people—just like he did when he *proposed* in front of those reporters—all to get himself a contract."

Paige looked like she was fighting a smile. "A tool?"

"Whatever. You know what I meant."

Paige cocked her head. "A hammer? A screwdriver? Maybe a socket wrench?"

"Stop." Liza shook her head. "I'm not in the mood to laugh." But she did grin a little. She glanced over at the opposite table where Cole had made his pies in their pie war. On it sat a cake that caught her eye.

Paige followed her line of vision and frowned. "That was supposed to be for your engagement."

"What is it?"

"A cake."

"I see that, but what *is* it?" Liza stepped to the other side of the kitchen to get a closer look. Paige trailed behind her.

"I had a baseball player cake mold that I use for kid's birthday cakes, so I fixed it up for you guys."

Paige used a Sugar Sheet overlay of a Nationals player in a batting stance, put Cole's number on the jersey and gave the guy blond hair. She'd even put a little mole on his cheek. Where the player's hands met the bat, she'd stuck a gumball-machine diamond ring.

Liza sniffled, trying not to tear up again.

"It was the best I could do on short notice," Paige said.

"Thank you, really. I should've guessed you'd do something thoughtful like that. I'm sorry you went to the trouble, considering…"

"No problem." Paige squinted at the cake, deep in thought. "Cole believes in voodoo magic, right?"

Liza had no idea where she was going with this. "Yes?"

Paige took the cake out to a table in the front, farthest away from her one customer. Liza followed her.

"Have a seat." Paige hurried back into the kitchen, and returned a few minutes later with two cups of espresso, plates and napkins, a knife, and a packet of pink-striped cake pop sticks.

Paige opened the cake pop sticks, handed several to Liza, and grinned mischievously. She took one herself and stabbed it into the cake, right on the baseball player's butt. "There's some voodoo magic for you, mister."

Liza couldn't help but laugh this time. Only Paige would've thought of something like this.

"Your turn," Paige said.

Liza picked up one of her sticks, hesitated, then poked the player in the eye. As juvenile as it was, she got a strange sort of satisfaction from it. She grabbed another stick and went for the knees. Before long, the cake looked like a pink-striped porcupine, and Paige had Liza laughing and sipping espresso.

"We got him pretty good," Paige said, cutting the cake amid all the voodoo sticks, and somehow managing to come out with a couple of pieces that were only partially mangled.

"Delicious," Liza murmured through a mouthful of almond-tinged pound cake that melted on her tongue.

Paige looked pleased. She might be the only person who doubted the deliciousness of anything she baked. "I know you don't want to hear this—"

Liza gave her an exaggerated frown. Just when she was

starting to cheer up…

"But I wouldn't be a very good friend if I didn't say it."

She looked at Paige skeptically, but she knew that wouldn't stop her.

"You and Cole both misled each other…at first. You started dating him because of a deal. I get why—even why you didn't tell me—but still. Frank might've told him to settle down if he wanted another contract with the Nats, but Cole didn't have to do what Frank said."

Liza scowled.

"Okay. Maybe, in the beginning, he might not have been a hundred percent sincere—even though I think he was into you all along. But there was nothing fake about the way he looked at you all starry-eyed. He's not an actor. He's a baseball player." Paige hurried to the kitchen and came back with four sections of newspaper, all featuring pictures of Liza and Cole, including the one from last night. She spread them across the table. "See? Look at him. Look at you. From the very beginning, it was there. That *it* that everyone dreams about finding. You two are in love, however you got there." She crossed her arms and gave Liza the Paige-stare. "*Both* of you."

Liza hated to admit it, but Paige had made some good points. If she hadn't known the couple in the pictures—hadn't been one of them—she would've bet they were in love, too.

"I understand why you reacted the way you did. I would've done the same thing." Paige stuck her finger in the icing, came away with a dollop, and ate it. "But think about it this way…if he was putting on an act, dating you just to get a contract from the Nats, he was doing a bang-up job already without having to freakin' propose. Jeez, he'd already skated by with a practice one. How was he gonna get out of that huge seventh-inning-stretch production if he was just faking it? That ring alone must've set him back a few fat paychecks. Sure, he's rich, but that was an investment he didn't need to make. Besides, how much negative publicity do you think he'd get for breaking it off with you after he went and made you the sweetheart of the World Series?"

She chewed on the icing end of one of the cake pop sticks. "And America doesn't want a sweetheart with puffy eyes and a naked ring finger. You should see what he has to say for himself. You didn't give him a chance last night."

"I blocked his number from my phone."

"Why?" Paige's eyes widened. "I would've at least wanted the satisfaction of seeing how many times he called or texted." She winked.

Liza gave her a wan grin. "You would." She took another bite of the sinfully good pound cake and promised herself she would go for a run later.

"Maybe you're afraid he'll have a good explanation for what he did and you just don't want to hear it."

Was Paige right? Liza had what she thought was a good explanation for making the deal with Frank, even though Cole might not like the idea. Then again, Cole probably felt the same way about his agreement with Frank.

"Maybe you're right," Liza said. "I'm so used to being alone—"

"And sad."

"And seeing my future like that." Things were becoming clearer in her mind—probably thanks to the sugar and caffeine. And to Paige. "So at the first sign of trouble with Cole, I bailed, and headed back to my comfort zone."

"That about covers it." Paige nodded, and a section of pink-striped hair fell in front of her shoulder. "Do you still like feeling that way, or did you like how you felt when you were with Cole?"

Liza's heart sank. She studied the barren spot on her finger where her engagement ring should've been, then picked the fake one off the cake and put it on. "Oh, God, Paige. What have I done?"

Chapter Twenty-One

Liza stepped into her office at the foundation, feeling better after spending yesterday with Paige. She'd pretty much gotten in the way while Paige baked to fulfill several large special orders. Paige had helped her work through the situation with Cole, and Liza had woken up this morning feeling better about things. She'd unblocked his number from her phone and made a pact with herself—if she didn't hear from him before lunchtime, she'd make the first move and call him. Or text? She still couldn't decide. And she had no idea yet what she would say or write.

She took off her jacket and draped it over a chair, catching a glance of her wall calendar. November already. Time had rushed by since she'd been with Cole. And the days had been happy ones, with all the late-season baseball and postseason play. With all of Cole's tender kisses and nights wrapped in his arms. Liza smiled a little. Should she even wait until lunchtime to call him?

She pulled her chair away from her desk and almost sat, but then noticed the white envelope that had been left on the seat. Her name was written on the front in handwriting that bordered on block lettering. She picked it up, opened it, and pulled out the paper inside—a blank page folded around a check from Frank Price, made out to the foundation in the amount of five hundred thousand dollars.

A tingly surge of adrenaline radiated through Liza. Her hands trembled and she sank onto the chair. Frank must have dropped the check off yesterday—or had a courier bring it—because Liza was the only person in the office so far this morning and probably would be until midday. She'd unlocked the door herself.

It had taken Frank only hours to make good on their deal. Had Cole told Frank to pay her off and be done with her? She hated to admit it, but she'd hoped Frank would make an argument that Cole had really wanted to date her, and had really fallen for her, too. But if Cole had been sincere about being with her—*being her husband*—then there would've been no need for Frank to have written the check at all.

Liza tossed the envelope on her desk and pressed her eyes closed. What little hope she had that things would work out had been dashed by the stroke of a pen. She felt even worse to have been let down a second time.

More camps, more kids, better equipment…

She thought of all the good a half-million dollars would do for BADD, but it was little comfort. Regardless of the good it would do, she couldn't take Frank's donation after all that had happened.

Maybe Paige could help her see a bright side to the situation, but Liza didn't have the energy to call her. Besides, she'd dumped on Paige all day yesterday. After hearing about the check, Paige might hurry over with another voodoo cake, and Liza didn't have the stomach for that this morning. She could, however, use some coffee.

She went into the kitchen where, while she'd been off

yesterday, her coworkers had posted all the newspaper pictures of her and Cole on the white board and written "Congratulations Liza!" in huge colorful letters. Someone had even drawn a giant diamond ring. Thank goodness they were all out working on the anti-doping video project that was wrapping up. How was she going to explain to them what had happened, and to everyone else? Especially her parents.

She brewed some coffee and went back to her office, determined to caffeinate herself and review the applications she'd received for summer camp attendees. Surprisingly, several hours passed while she read the touching stories in silence.

Around eleven, she heard someone come in the front door. Moments later, her mom called from the hallway. "It's me, sweetie."

Her mom came into her office, looking a little tired but still lovely in tailored black slacks and a spice-orange jacket. The woman was a true-blue Orioles fan, Series win or not. Liza felt for her parents. They'd had such high hopes for the team, then the disappointment of coming so close and losing. She didn't have the heart to pile on with more disappointing news. For today, she'd have to fake it.

"Hi, Mom." Liza hugged her tightly. "You doing okay? And Dad?"

"We're all right." Her mom nodded. "Looking ahead to next season now."

"Go Os." Liza's words sounded flat.

Her mom glanced out the window at the last of the leaves falling from the ginkgo trees in the courtyard, and Frank's check caught her eye.

Crap. Liza had meant to put it away, then mail it back to Frank.

"Good gracious." Her mom picked up the check. "Frank

Price gave us five hundred thousand dollars?"

Liza shrugged one shoulder and smiled as if she were excited. "Wow, huh?"

"Wow is right." Her mom shook her head. "Poor Frank is really trying to make amends, isn't he? Tell you what, put this in your purse and we'll take it to the bank on our way back from lunch."

"Lunch?" Liza couldn't imagine keeping up this act during a long Friday afternoon lunch with her mom. But the alternative was staying here and facing her coworkers even sooner.

"Naomi Tyler just opened a little bistro in Middleburg so I thought we'd check it out. You know, a little mother-daughter engagement celebration lunch." Her mom's eyes glimmered.

"That's quite a drive for lunch."

"So take the afternoon off—my treat." Her mom ran the place, so Liza could hardly say no. She didn't care about appearances right now. And this way, she could avoid her coworkers altogether. Until Monday.

"And what's a little drive when there's so much to talk about?" Her mom beamed. "We've got a wedding to plan."

Liza rubbed her forehead where a headache was setting in.

Her mom's gaze followed Liza's hand. "Where's that gorgeous ring?"

Liza's heart skipped ahead a few beats. "Getting sized." She hated lying to her mom.

"Then it will fit just right." Her mom smiled.

Lisa turned away and got busy shutting down her computer and gathering her coat and purse. Given enough time to look closely, her mom would figure out that nothing was just right anymore. Just right was just a fairy tale.

They locked up the office, headed out, and got in her

mom's car. Liza quickly put on her sunglasses to hide her eyes. But her mom was distracted enough by traffic, wedding ideas, and plans for Frank's donation, that Liza didn't have to try too hard to play along. She could tell that, as excited as her mom was about the idea of a wedding, she was treading lightly with the subject. They'd already planned one for Liza and Wes. Without coming out and saying it, her mom seemed uncertain how similar Liza would want her and Cole's big day to be. No worries there, really. Neither wedding was ever going to happen.

Liza had thought a drive in the rolling countryside on a gorgeous fall day would soothe her soul a little. And it did. Until she realized that she and Cole had traveled this way together a couple of times, back and forth to the storybook farm. Liza's chest tightened.

"I promised Charlene Shelton I would swing by and drop off a program from the Series." Her mom's voice still sounded sad when she mentioned it. She gestured to the backseat where several programs were stacked along with a few folded sections of newspaper. Liza hoped they weren't the ones with pictures of her and Cole. From now until forever, she'd have an aversion to newspapers. They were good for nothing but lining birdcages and house-training a puppy.

"Who is Charlene Shelton?" Liza asked. Her mom and dad knew so many people that Liza couldn't keep them all straight.

"Jim's wife."

"Which Jim?"

"Your dad's golf buddy Jim. He and Charlene were in Pinehurst during the Series. Their place is just up the road."

Great. Now Liza would have more people to fake it with.

The area began to look even more familiar with the hilly fields and woodlands. White fences seemed to stretch for miles as they passed horse farms and estates that appeared even more idyllic beneath the bright turquoise sky. Her mom slowed and made a turn into a long drive bordered with rows of magnolia trees. It took Liza a second to realize it, but this was *the* farm. The place Cole had taken her twice. The place where he'd first said he loved her.

"Jim and Charlene are Nats fans?" Liza asked, remembering the curly Ws embroidered on the cushions on the chairs by the pond.

Her mom smiled knowingly. "We forgive them."

So Cole knew Jim and Charlene, too. This was going to be worse than Liza had thought. Charlene would be raving over their engagement.

Instead of turning toward the barn, where Liza and Cole had gone when they'd come here, her mom kept straight down the driveway. Soon a house came into view. And not just any house, but an incredible stone and white clapboard farmhouse with two chimneys and a sweeping front porch.

"Wow, their house is gorgeous. This whole place is like…" Liza couldn't think of the words she wanted. "…a country estate paradise." With the red-and-white barn that she knew about but couldn't see from here, the fire pit next to the pond, the party lights along the pier. Everything about this place was perfect…except those curly W chair cushions.

Her mom pulled around the stone-paved circle in front of the house and parked.

"How about I wait in the car?" As much as Liza wanted to see inside that house, she didn't want to have to talk about Cole. Especially on the very property where their romance had begun. She rubbed her stomach. "I'm kind of hungry. Maybe you could just drop and dash."

"We won't be long, I promise." Her mom grabbed a World Series program and one of the sections of newspaper from the backseat. "I'm sure Charlene wants to congratulate you."

Great.

Liza reluctantly picked up her purse and got out of the car. Until she worked up the nerve to tell people what had happened, or until everyone learned it from Cole, she'd have to play along. She and her mom stepped onto the front porch where large pots of yellow mums bloomed like bursts of sunshine between sets of white rocking chairs, and flanked the deep-red front door. A cool fall breeze rustled the colorful leaves that had fallen from a giant oak tree in the front yard.

Her mom rang the doorbell, then glanced at the newspaper in her hand and sighed. "I grabbed the wrong one." She hurried off the porch just as the front door opened.

With a weary half-smile on her face, Liza looked up and straight into Cole's bright blue eyes.

• • •

After being without Liza for the last couple of days, Cole had to restrain himself from taking her into his arms right that second. He'd missed everything about her, and the peace he'd felt just knowing she was his. His chest tightened. She *wasn't* his anymore. Man, he hoped he could convince her to give him another chance. Life without her would be a million kinds of miserable. That was painfully clear to him now.

She stood in front of him, looking tired but simply beautiful in her charcoal-gray pantsuit. The surprised look on her face was priceless. She shook her head, her eyes still wide, and let her purse slide onto the porch. "What are you doing here?" she asked quietly, sounding dazed.

Cole stepped onto the porch and closed the door behind him. He risked taking her hand, and she didn't pull away. A surge of relief pulsed through him. Just touching her again gave him hope. The porch wrapped around the house and he led her to the front corner where the view was most spectacular. As crazy as it was, his legs had gone a little rubbery, so he leaned against the railing. "I live here."

It took Liza a second to get it. "This is *your* farm?"

He nodded.

"Your barn…your pond…your party lights?"

He smiled a little. Of all the things she might think of, she'd mentioned the party lights. She saw things from a different perspective, and he loved her for that, plus so many other reasons. "Yep. I'm the friend of Mack's who owns this farm. I wanted to wait until after we were engaged to tell you—kinda like an engagement surprise." He shrugged. "But that didn't work out so well." Cole tried to sound casual to cover all the hurt he'd been feeling since he lost her. He'd tried to get angry about the deal she'd made with Frank—and managed to for about five minutes. But ultimately he couldn't see where she'd done anything worse than he had.

The sun glinted off the tears welling in Liza's eyes.

He smoothed his thumb across her fingers, waiting for her to say something.

"Just so you know," she said softly, "if you're ever thinking about it sometime…I regret making that deal with Frank. No one should gain from being disingenuous, even for a good cause. I'm sorry if you got hurt."

"What I did was worse," he said, "because it was totally selfish." The breeze caught a lock of her hair and blew it across her face. He gently brushed it aside and tucked it behind her ear, lingering near her earlobe, then trailing his fingers down her silky-smooth neck. His throat tightened. How could he live without this woman?

"And just so you know," he said, "if you're ever thinking about it sometime…from the moment I got to know the real

Liza, and every second since, I've wanted you to be my wife." He took a deep breath and exhaled loudly. "And not because of a contract." His pulse thrummed in his ears. "I don't want a new contract if I can't have you."

Liza lowered her eyebrows and gazed at him intently.

"If you think I've been pretending," he said, "I haven't. I pretended with every girl I ever dated, and it was a hell of a lonely life. Then there was you. The girl who actually *got* me. Who knew my past and didn't judge me. Who saw my flaws and stuck around anyway. Who sparked a crazy chemistry I'd never felt before." He clutched both of her hands in his. "Who overcame her own grief and gave me a chance."

She blinked back tears and shifted her gaze toward the sprawling farmland.

Cole cleared his throat. This kind of talk was so far beyond his comfort zone. "And you like baseball nearly as much as I do."

She nodded. "That's true."

"Before you, baseball was the love of my life. But you mean more to me than baseball ever could." He clenched his jaw. "So I gave it up."

Liza narrowed her eyes. "What?"

Cole reached into the back pocket of his jeans and pulled out a rolled-up page from that day's sports section of the *Washington Post*. He handed it to Liza and pointed out the headline: "Nationals' Collins Opts Out."

She shook her head and read aloud, "After his selection as World Series MVP, All-Star first baseman Cole Collins shocked the Nationals with the news that he is not interested in renewing his contract with the franchise, or any other major league team."

She stared at Cole, dumbfounded.

He took the newspaper from her, set it on a nearby

rocking chair, and took her hands in his. No doubt he was setting a new record for sustained adrenaline surges. He was more nervous now than he'd been during his proposal at the World Series in front of all those people. But this time it was just him and Liza. And even more than last time, everything was on the line.

He got down on one knee and gazed up into her eyes. "I want you to marry me, and never doubt it was *you* I wanted and nothing else." He reached into his shirt pocket, pulled out the sparkling engagement ring, and nestled it in the palm of his hand. "This represents my heart." He fumbled in his pocket again, came out with a larger ring, and set it next to the other one. "This one, my life. I want to give both of them to you. Please say you'll marry me."

• • •

Reeling with emotion, Liza stared at the big ring Cole held next to the diamond—a man's brushed-platinum signet ring with a polished curly W on it.

"What's this?" she asked, nerves twisting her insides and making her shaky.

"The Nats organization gave us those after we won the Series. They said it could hold the place on our fingers until we get the official rings in the spring." He smiled sadly.

Liza thought she might lose it right then. Struggling to keep herself together, she tugged his free hand until he got the message and stood up. The stunned look on his face nearly broke her heart. She took his other hand and closed his fingers around the rings. "I'm sorry, Cole."

He grimaced but still managed to look handsome. She thought she might've seen tears in his eyes but he managed to blink them back quickly. It took all of her self-control not to wrap her arms around him, but she had to make things right first.

"I believe you, but I can't be the reason you quit the game you love." She cupped his scruffy face in her hand. "Will you tell the Nats you want a new contract, and then marry me?"

His slow and easy grin told her what she wanted to know before he even said it. He kissed her tenderly and whispered, "Yes."

Her heart soared as he slid her engagement ring onto her finger, and she put the Nats ring on his. This was good practice for exchanging wedding rings, which couldn't happen soon enough for her.

The moment the rings were on their fingers the front door opened. Liza turned as her mom rushed out onto the porch followed by her dad, Mack and Brenda, Frank, and Paige.

She looked at them wide-eyed, her mouth agape. "Y'all set me up," she teased. It was touching that they'd all come together to reunite her and Cole. She couldn't think of a time she'd ever felt more loved.

"We all need a little nudging now and then," her mom said.

"And no one told me this was Cole's farm." Liza fixed Frank with a playfully sharp look, then shifted her gaze to Mack and Brenda.

"We had our orders," Mack said sheepishly.

"Mack and Brenda live here, too," Cole said. He pointed toward the woods in the opposite direction of the barn and the pond. "Down that way about a half mile. They take care of the place for me." He put his arm around Liza and pulled her close. "For us. Been doing it for a couple of years now."

For us...

"I couldn't have picked better neighbors," Liza said.

"Glad to see you kids got everything straight." Frank rocked back and forth on his feet.

Cole raised his eyebrows. "Not everything." With just two words, he had everyone's attention. "Liza won't marry me unless I tell the Nats I want a new contract."

Liza saw the relief on Frank's face—and everyone else's, too.

"Well I'm glad *someone* could talk some sense into you," Frank said to Cole.

Her dad gave Cole a congratulatory pat on the back. "If that Nats thing doesn't work out for you, there's this team up the beltway…" He smiled.

Cole nodded, looking humble. "I'd be honored."

"There's one more thing." Liza grabbed her purse, took out Frank's check, and handed it to him. "No deal." She rested her head against Cole's shoulder.

Frank glanced at the check and handed it back to her. "Keep the money. It's for a good cause."

"For real?" she asked, astonished.

Frank nodded.

"Thank you." Her mom hugged him, beaming.

"Yes," Liza said, "thank you all for everything." She stood on tiptoes and kissed Cole. "We couldn't have done this without you."

"This is fun and all," Paige said. "But we've got a picnic lunch waiting down by the pond." She winked at Liza. "And I made you a new cake without holes in it."

"Mmm. Sounds delicious." Liza gazed at Cole, still amazed by all that had happened. "So this is going to be our place now?"

He nodded, his eye practically dancing.

"Our barn…our pond…our Adirondack chairs?"

He grinned crookedly. "Yes."

"Then we're definitely going to have to do something about those cushions."

Acknowledgments

I had so much fun writing *The Practice Proposal* because it takes place in a world I love—the world of Major League Baseball and the Washington Nationals. I hope I have brought it to life for you the way they bring it alive for me. My days are always a little brighter during baseball season.

Special thanks to my amazing editors Stacy Abrams and Alycia Tornetta, for taking a chance with this one and having the patience to see it through. I stay (somewhat) sane in this crazy writer's life thanks to the unwavering support and good humor of my author friends Kelsey Browning, Tracey Devlyn, Adrienne Giordano, and Nancy Naigle. You girls are the best!

My mom deserves a special mention for all the times I rushed her off the phone when I was on deadline, and for her love and moral support. And there are no words to properly thank my husband, Mike, for his patience, his wacky perspective, his willingness to eat sandwiches for dinner (a lot), and his happily-ever-after kind of love.

About the Author

Award-winning author Tracy March writes romantic thrillers influenced by her career in the pharmaceutical field and her interest in science and politics. She also writes lighthearted romances inspired by her real-life happily ever after.

Always up for travel and adventure, Tracy has flown in a stunt plane, snowmobiled on the Continental Divide, zip-lined in the Swiss Alps, and been chased by a bull in the mountains of St. Lucia. She loves Nationals baseball, Saturday date nights, and Dairy Queen Blizzards—and rarely goes a day without Diet Coke and Cheez-Its.

Tracy lives in Yorktown, Virginia, with her superhero husband who works for NASA. They recently spent two years living in Washington, DC, and enjoy visiting often—especially when the Nats are in town.

Tracy is also the author of the romantic thriller Girl Three, available now. Visit her online at www.TracyMarch.com

Find your Bliss with **Ophelia London's** *Speaking of Love...*

She was still staring at the big house with the red roof. Okay, so the outside was built of split logs, but could that really qualify it as a log cabin? She climbed out of the truck, slid the back of the seat forward, and reached for her bag.

"I'll take care of that," Rick said. He was suddenly standing right behind her. His nearness startled her, but it also felt like a blanket of warmth wrapped around her body.

"I can carry it," she protested automatically, trying to haul out the heavy bag, but it was caught on something.

"I know you can," he said. "But I need you to unlock the front door. My hands are full." He lifted his arms out to his sides, displaying that he was already carrying the cooler and his own bag. "The keys are in my pocket," he said. "If you don't mind."

Mac looked down at the front of his jeans and swallowed. "Umm…"

"Just pull them out, Mac," Rick said, and then added, "I dare you."

She looked up at him. He was grinning. "Rick, I…"

"I'm just playing around," he said, laughing. "But my hands are starting to freeze. Seriously, you need my keys to unlock the door."

"I'm not going in…there," she said, her eyes involuntarily flicking to the area in question.

"Mac," Rick said. "We're both adults here. We've been traveling for three hours. Aren't you ready to go inside?"

She blinked about a million times, staring straight at the

bulge in his jeans. She felt like she was about to faint. When did you become such a prude? one part of her brain asked. It's Rick. Yeah, another part of her brain chimed in. Exactly. It's Rick.

"Hello?" he said, breaking into her over-heating thoughts. "Impending frostbite happening here."

"Fine," she said. "Just…hold still." She could tell he was grinning again. She could feel it, even though she refused to look at his face.

In order to go ahead with the delicate procedure, she had to step right up to him, closer than when they had shared a slow dance on their first non-date. Thinking of that moment wasn't helping Mac's concentration.

Feeling the warmth of his body directly in front of her, she took in a deep breath and gingerly slid her fingers inside his pocket, biting her lip in concentration. She could hear his breathing shallow, just like hers had. With the tip of her finger, she felt the cold touch of the metal key ring. Holding her breath, she curled one finger around it and pulled it free of his pocket. She felt Rick's warm breath on her cheek. While still standing before him, she looked up, not knowing what she should do next…even though the natural impulse was almost blinding.

The way Rick was grinning made her blush furiously.

"What a champ." Then he actually winked. "Here, take this," he said, holding out the cooler to her. I'll grab yours."

Mac took it, then stepped back as Rick hauled her bag from behind the seat.

"So, was that one of your moves? The pocket thing?" she asked, feeling like she needed to lay face-down in the snow for a while to cool off.

"It will be if it worked."

Find your Bliss with Cindi Madsen's *Falling for Her Fiance*

Dani caught a whiff of cologne, musky and woodsy, with a mixture of outdoors and even sweat. It shouldn't have smelled good to her, but it made a flutter go through her chest. Her gaze traveled up Wes's muscled arms, well-built pecs, and settled on his face. She found herself thinking about all of his good qualities. How she'd never find a guy as good as him to date. How stupid Sophie was for dumping him.

I guess I'm stupid for not dating him myself.

Then she remembered how their one attempt to move the slightest bit past friends had not only crashed and burned but also nearly ruined their friendship.

He really is the whole package, though.

Wes's eyebrows drew together. "What? Why are you looking at me like that?"

She glanced away, heat rising in her cheeks. "Just thinking."

"About what?"

She met his eyes, telling herself it didn't mean anything that her stomach lurched. "Just about today. Being here with you. It's the most fun I've had in a long time."

He put his hand on her bare leg and squeezed. "Right back at you. And I'm glad your knee surgery hasn't slowed you down. When I first saw the cut, I thought you'd never be able to walk normally again, much less play ball."

All her blood seemed to rush to where his hand was warming her skin and she suddenly had to work at getting words to come out of her mouth. "Well, if I hadn't had you there to help me recover, I probably would've pushed myself too hard and never fully healed."

Wes brushed his fingers across the scar on her knee, and her leg involuntarily twitched at his touch. She hoped he didn't notice.

She wished she didn't. But her heart was beating faster, and the way he was running his fingertips along her knee was sending little zips of heat across her skin.

Pull it together, Dani. He's your best friend. Don't screw it up now because you've gone without so much as a hug from a guy in months.

She swung her feet to the ground and stood so fast sparks of light danced across her vision. "I'm beat. I'm gonna go to bed."

She waved—cursing herself for the stupid, awkward gesture—and rushed back to the bedroom. Closing the door, she shook her head.

What the hell was that all about? Even though she knew she'd never be able to sleep, she crawled into bed. Wes's bed.

Earlier today, she'd been right there with him when he'd said they were friends and would never be more. So why was she noticing the way he smelled, and why was her skin humming under his touch? Why was she suddenly so aware of the fact that Wes usually slept where she was now?

Find your Bliss with these new releases...

Just for the Summer by **Jenna Rutland**

Dani Sullivan has come to Lake Bliss to write her latest cookbook…and to see if the baby she gave up for adoption eight years ago is happy. But when she sees her little boy—indeed happy despite living with his single dad—she finds she can't keep her promise to stay away…from her son *or* from his flirtatious father, Matt, who has no idea of her true identity. But when Matt learns Dani's secrets, will he still want her to stay? Or will her chance for love last just for the summer?

His Reluctant Rancher by **Roxanne Snopek**

The last place city girl Desiree Burke expected to find herself was living at and working on a ranch, much less butting heads with the ranch's sexy cowboy owner, Zach Gamble. Zach's been through a traumatic car accident, and he doesn't believe he deserves to find love again. But as Des works her way into his ranch, his family, and his life, suddenly the last person who belonged there is the only one he believes belongs…with him.

Playing the Maestro by **Aubrie Dionne**

Melody Mires has sworn off dating musicians, but when the sexy European conductor Wolf Braun takes over her struggling symphony, her hesitation almost flies out the window—until he opens his mouth. Wolf is arrogant, haughty, *and* her boss. Dating is out of the question, but as their feelings reach a fever pitch, can they risk both their careers for a chance at love?

Real Men Don't Quit by Coleen Kwan

When famous author Luke Maguire decides to write his next novel in the small town of Burronga, Australia, he's sure he can ignore Tyler, the fiery redhead next door. Only Tyler and Luke can't stay away from each other. So they set rules. No staying overnight, no future plans, no sappy good-byes when Luke inevitably quits town. But the chemistry between them is too strong to contain in a rulebook. Are Luke and Tyler ready to risk their lives of independence for something more?

Tempting Cameron by Karen Erickson

For Cameron McKenzie, resident good girl Chloe Dawson has always just been his younger sister Jane's best friend. It isn't until Jane's wedding that Chloe reappears in his life — and the beautiful woman now tempts him beyond reason. Chloe's always dreamed of a future with the dark, brooding Cam, so she makes him an offer: one sweet summer romance with no strings attached. This good girl's ready for an adventure — one that just might last a lifetime.

CPSIA information can be obtained
at www.ICGtesting.com
Printed in the USA
LVHW080259230821
695880LV00014B/709